The Lady Grace
Mysteries

From the Daybookes
of Lady Grace Cavendish

Book the Fifth

Exile

The Lady Grace Mysteries from Delacorte Press

ASSASSIN
BETRAYAL
CONSPIRACY
DECEPTION
EXILE

The Lady Grace Mysteries from Delacorte Press

ASSASSIN
BETRAYAL
CONSPIRACY
DECEPTION
EXILE

The Lady

Myster

From the D

of Lady Grace

Book the

Ex

THE Lady Grace MYSTERIES

From the Daybookes of Lady Grace Cavendish

BOOK THE FIFTH

EXILE

Jan Burchett and Sara Vogler are writing as Grace Cavendish

DELACORTE PRESS

Published by
Delacorte Press
an imprint of
Random House Children's Books
a division of Random House, Inc.
New York

Series created by Working Partners Ltd.
Text copyright © 2006 by Working Partners Ltd.

Visit us on the Web! www.randomhouse.com/kids
Educators and librarians, for a variety of teaching tools, visit us at
www.randomhouse.com/teachers

Library of Congress Cataloging-in-Publication Data
Burchett, Jan.
Exile / Jan Burchett and Sara Vogler are writing as Grace Cavendish.
p. cm. — (The Lady Grace mysteries, from the daybookes of
Lady Grace Cavendish ; book the fifth)
Summary: Thirteen-year-old Lady Grace Cavendish, maid of honor to Queen
Elizabeth I, describes in her diary how she tries to discover who stole a
magical ruby belonging to the visiting princess of Sharakand.
ISBN 0-385-73322-4 (trade : alk. paper) — ISBN 0-385-90341-3 (glb : alk. paper)
[1. Princesses—Fiction. 2. Jewelry—Fiction. 3. Kings, queens, rulers, etc.—Fiction.
4. Great Britain—History—Elizabeth, 1558–1603—Fiction. 5. Diaries—Fiction.
6. Mystery and detective stories.] I. Vogler, Sara. II. Title. III. Series.
PZ7 .B915965Exi 2006
[Fic]—dc22
2005006542

The text of this book is set in 13-point Cloister.
Book design by Trish Parcell Watts
Printed in the United States of America
February 2006
10 9 8 7 6 5 4 3 2 1
BVG

*For Deborah Smith, with love and thanks
for helping Lady Grace Cavendish become
Her Majesty's Lady Pursuivant*

MOST PRIVY AND SECRETE

DAYBOOKE THE FIFTH OF

MY LADY GRACE CAVENDISH,

MAID OF HONOUR TO HER GRACIOUS MAJESTY

QUEEN ELIZABETH I OF THAT NAME

AT THE PRESENCE CHAMBER OF HER MAJESTY

PALACE OF PLACENTIA,

GREENWICH

ALL MISCREANTS AND ILL-THINKERS, KEEP OUT

Exile

The Queen's Presence Chamber
Late morning

I am sitting with the other Maids of Honour,
awaiting the Queen. We are huddled as close to the
roaring fire as we can get without scorching our
skirts. I must be especially careful for Mrs.
Champernowne, the Mistress of the Maids, has
warned that there is not an endless supply of kirtles
for me. (The last one only had a little tear from my
recent entanglement with a holly bush and I did not
mean to put my foot through the hole!)

We are not usually at the Palace of Placentia at
this season. We moved here in a rush, for there was
talk of plague near Whitehall last month, where we
were to have spent the winter. I think it was just a
rumour, for plague generally strikes in summer, but
Her Majesty has a horror of it. So there was nothing

1

for it but we must pack everything up and come to Greenwich.

Mrs. Champernowne has left instructions that we are to do our embroidery and listen dutifully while Mary Shelton reads to us from "A Godly Meditation of the Christian Soul," by Marguerite of Angoulême. It is the Queen's own translation, done when she was only fifteen, and I am sure it is excellent—but Marguerite of Angoulême is a little too Godly for my taste.

I am pleased to write in my new daybooke. It is a beautiful book with a pink vellum cover, and a gift from Her Majesty herself for the New Year. I must be certain I do not make ink blots over it. But that will be hard, for I have exciting news!

Today a most unusual guest arrives at the palace—Banoo Yasmine of Sharakand! "Banoo" means "Lady," for Banoo Yasmine is from a noble family and said to be very beautiful. Sharakand is thousands of miles away near the Holy Lands. No one at Court has ever visited it, but the stories are many and the Maids are chattering of exotic clothes, strange animals, and fruit to be picked from the trees all year round. Banoo Yasmine is an exile from this wondrous place and Her Majesty has offered her sanctuary. I must be sure that no one peeks over my shoulder as I write, for only I of all the Maids know the reason for the Banoo's exile. It is most entertaining to listen to their fanciful ideas on the subject.

"I have heard she is a great sorceress!" said Penelope. "Mayhap she has upset someone by turning them into an earwig."

"I am certain that she must have fled on account of a prince of Araby," Lady Sarah Bartelmy told us all with a flick of her copper curls. "He wanted to steal her away because he was smitten with love for her."

Lady Sarah thinks of nothing but love and marriage.

"That could be true," agreed Mary Shelton, "for her beauty is legendary. She will surely win all the men's hearts here at Court."

That, however, did not please my fine Lady Sarah, for she considers herself to be the most beautiful of the Maids and does not like any sniff of competition. "No one has yet seen her!" she snapped. "I warrant that in truth she is really ugly and has cast an enchantment on those who look at her! That would be how she caught the eye of the prince of Araby."

"Perhaps you should try that, Sarah," said Lady Jane Coningsby, very sweetly.

Lady Jane and Lady Sarah see themselves as rivals

for the affections of all the young unmarried gentlemen at Court and cannot be friends. But before Lady Sarah could make a barbed reply there were shrieks from Carmina and Penelope.

"We must not be unkind about the Banoo!" exclaimed Carmina. "Or she may cast a spell on us!"

"She could turn us into frogs!" giggled Penelope.

"Or crows!" squealed Carmina. "Or even pigs!"

They rocked with laughter till I thought they would fall off their cushions.

"In truth," I said solemnly, "the Banoo will not need to turn you into any beast."

"Why not?" asked Mary.

"Because she will bring her own fabulous creatures with her," I told them, trying not to laugh.

"What are they?" gasped Carmina and Penelope in one breath.

"Huge birds that can carry a man on their wings, fearsome snakes, and giant lizards with two heads," I said. "And they are all her enemies under enchantment. Now I must begin my new daybooke before Her Majesty arrives. It will please her to see me writing in it."

I wish that the Banoo's story was as exotic as the Maids imagine. Alas, it is rather sad. The Queen told me the real reason for Banoo Yasmine's visit some weeks ago when her messenger came with letters asking for sanctuary.

"Keep your counsel until the Banoo's arrival, Grace," she bade me. "For the other Maids are too apt to gossip. They would work themselves into a great ferment over the matter and I have not the patience to bear it."

The Queen often confides in me, for she knows I am her loyal subject and would not break her confidence. I have been at Court since my birth, and the Queen is my godmother. Both my parents are dead. My father died just after I was born and two years ago my dear mother drank poisoned wine intended for the Queen, thus saving Her Majesty's life but losing her own. I am the youngest Maid of Honour in Her Majesty's service, and secretly—it still gives me a thrill to write it—I am her Lady Pursuivant. That means it is my duty to seek out wrongdoers and those who wish her ill.

But I am wandering from my story. The Queen told me that the Banoo comes from a noble family which has served the kings of Sharakand for centuries. The head of the family has always been the king's Chief Minister, rather as Secretary Cecil is to our Queen.

And so it has been for hundreds of years. But now

all is changed. There has been a revolt. The old king was murdered by a usurper who took the throne by force. The new king, Ashraf, declared the Banoo's family to be traitors and had them killed! Only Banoo Yasmine escaped. She fled Sharakand with a few of her loyal servants and her horses. She hopes to find a safe home in England, and so she comes to ask our Queen for sanctuary and for a loan, since the new king has stolen so much of her land and wealth that she is left quite poor! She will have to provide the Queen with surety for the loan, of course—something of a similar value that the Queen will hold in her safekeeping until the loan is repaid. But the Banoo still has many jewels—and mayhap some fabulous beasts or items of sorcery that are not to be found in all of England!

Still, the Banoo's tale is a sad one. If only I could persuade the Queen to send me to Sharakand as her Lady Pursuivant to find a way to overthrow the evil new king! I but recently solved the mystery of the dead body at the Frost Fair, and once stowed away on a ship—though 'twas by accident—to rescue Lady Sarah from a wicked sea captain! Surely the evil King Ashraf could soon be overcome. I would arrive at the palace, after a long, hot journey by camel across the desert sands and—

A few minutes later

I had to break off my writing. The other Maids were laughing at me!

"What were you doing, Grace?" giggled Mary. "You stared into space, then started writing away, then you jiggled about on your cushion, then wrote some more."

"I wager you have a flea!" declared Lady Sarah, moving her skirts away from mine.

They would have laughed even more if I had said I was imagining a ride on a camel, so I made great play of scratching and searching for the flea.

"I had better not kill it," I said, seriously. "It could be Banoo Yasmine's advisor under an enchantment, sent ahead to find out what we are like!"

"Then I wish we could turn him back into a man!" declared Lady Jane. "He could answer all our questions."

"I would have him tell us about the Heart of Kings ruby," breathed Carmina.

At this all the Maids sighed in wonder, for we have all heard of the fabulous jewel owned by the Banoo. It is a legendary gem and the stories about it abound.

"It is said to be the most beautiful ruby in the world," declared Penelope.

"It is a perfect heart shape," added Lady Sarah, "and as big as a hen's egg. I would love to wear such a gorgeous thing."

"I would be too scared!" gasped Penelope. "For did not a powerful old magician conjure it up? I have heard it was given as a gift to Banoo Yasmine's family centuries ago and is protected with a spell. Evil will befall anyone who comes upon it unjustly!"

"So beware, dear Lady Sarah," murmured Lady Jane. "We would not wish to have evil befall you because you wore a bewitched jewel."

Lady Sarah scowled at her but Lady Jane merely smiled innocently.

"Listen!" I broke in.

All the Maids looked puzzled.

"To what?" asked Mary.

I put my ear to my elbow. "Can you not hear?" I said. "It is His Excellency, the Flea of Sharakand! He says he has never heard such nonsense in his life!"

Everybody—except Lady Jane—burst out laughing. And this time Carmina did fall off her cushion. But she could not have chosen a worse moment, for we heard the harbingers calling, "The Queen! The Queen!" and almost immediately the doors to the Privy Chamber burst open and Her Majesty swept in, followed by Secretary Cecil. We stopped laughing and jumped up to curtsy. Poor Carmina was sprawled on the floor and had to scrabble to her feet in a most ungainly fashion.

Her Majesty always makes a grand entrance. Today she is wearing a gown of vermilion, with sleeves decorated by the finest black and gold roses. She has strings of pearls around her neck and matching jewels adorning her fiery red hair. But it is not just the clothes that make her so imposing. She could wear a sack and we would all be on our knees in awe.

"Forgive these foolish wenches, Mr. Cecil," said the Queen grimly. "We are sure that they will now sit quietly as befits their station and give us peace so we may attend to our matters of state."

Mary Shelton quickly opened the "Godly Meditation" and began to read again. I have no wish to repeat the words, for I can say here in the privacy of my own daybooke that they are passing tedious. I will pick up my embroidery. I am attempting a robin redbreast and hoped to have him ready for the yuletide festivities but I forgot him and he was not finished in time. I shall see if I can finish him before next Christmas instead.

*In my bedchamber, just two
of the afternoon*

Mary Shelton, Lady Sarah, and I are in our bedchamber making ready for the arrival of the Banoo.
Just moments ago, several gentlemen of the Court
left through the archway on the waterfront and gal-
loped off east along the river. The Banoo must be
almost here, for they are her welcome party! As
usual, Mary and I are ready and waiting. Lady Sarah
cannot decide what stomacher to wear. As if anybody will notice if it is adorned with flowers or birds!
The young gentlemen of the Court are usually far
too busy gazing upon her bosom to look at her stomacher! But perhaps my fine lady is anxious that they
will only have eyes for the Banoo.

Mary is making patient suggestions and is being
snapped at for her trouble. I am sitting on my trunk
keeping out of the way as Lady Sarah flaps by like an
agitated goose.

I did not get far with my embroidery this morning.
In fact my poor little robin had a nasty shock, for I
dropped my bottle of ink on him! When I tried to
wipe the ink off, my daybooke fell to the floor of the
Presence Chamber with a terrible clatter.

"Lady Grace Cavendish!" exclaimed the Queen, glaring at me. "Come to my side at once."

I quickly gathered up my daybooke and embroidery and hastened to Her Majesty. I dropped a deep curtsy and waited to be chided.

"I have a fancy for apple tart at dinner," she said, to my astonishment—this did not sound like a rebuke! "I pray you go to the Privy Kitchen and make my wishes known, for I would eat within the hour."

I could have jumped up and down in delight that Her Majesty was thus enabling me to escape the boring matters of state—she could easily have sent a page to the kitchen. But I did not. Instead, "At once!" I exclaimed, and curtsied my way out as quickly as I could. I am sure that the Queen was trying hard not to smile at my enthusiasm. She raised a handkerchief to hide her mouth but her eyes were dancing. When I got to the Privy Kitchen, Mistress Berry, the head cook's wife, stared at me in surprise as I told her the Queen's order.

"But my lady," she said, "Jenny has had the apple tarts ready this past hour or more. Her Majesty gave the instruction last night!"

So my suspicions were correct. The Queen must

have seen my boredom and sent me off deliberately. She can be very thoughtful that way. Or mayhap she couldn't stand the disruptions I was causing.

"Still," Mistress Berry went on, "there are some trout pasties ready and cooling, and you have a hungry look about you."

I needed no persuasion. The pasties smelt delicious. She wrapped some in a linen cloth and handed them to me.

My errand was done. I skipped out of the kitchen and ran straight into my dear friend Ellie, who had her arms full of linen shirts. As usual I had to pretend to give her some order or other so that we could talk, for I am not supposed to be friends with a lowly laundrymaid. It makes me very cross, for a truer friend I could not have. The Queen knows of our friendship and should not condone it, but she can become remarkably blind or deaf when it suits her.

I had not seen Ellie since we moved from Whitehall, and we had much to catch up on. "Can you come with me?" I asked. "We could find Masou. I have trout pasties and more than enough for three."

Ellie's eyes lit up. She is small and thin and always hungry. It worries me that she doesn't get enough to eat. "Let me put these shirts in the starching room first," she said. "And then I can slip out for a moment."

We had quite a search for Masou. He was not in the tumblers' quarters—where he is often to be found practising with the rest of the troupe—or in the Great Hall, or in any of the pantries or workrooms.

To our great surprise we finally found him outside in the orchard, walking on his hands on the frozen ground and juggling balls with his feet. Masou's father brought him to England from Africa when he was very young, but although he has been here a long time he still complains that our climate is too cold for him. He does not venture out of doors in the winter if he can help it, so something must have been amiss.

"How now, Masou!" called Ellie as she spotted him. "What are you doing all topsy-turvy in the cold?"

Masou did a handspring and landed at our feet. "My ladies," he said, sweeping an elegant bow. "I am merely perfecting my art. Do you not know that the beauteous Banoo Yasmine will be arriving today from Sharakand, and the tumblers must be at their most splendid?"

"Well, you can give your hands a rest and come and wrap them round a pasty," said Ellie, nudging me. "Dish them up, Grace. I'm starving!"

I gave them a pasty each and we ran off to the herb garden and found our usual hiding place—inside the old yew hedge. It was warm and cosy and we knew no one would find us. We huddled together as we ate. Ellie sat in the middle as she never has enough clothes to keep warm.

"Where is this Sharakand?" she asked. "It sounds a goodly way off."

"'Tis in the south, where the sun shines all year," said Masou wistfully. "It lies between Persia and the Caspian Sea. I was there once with my father. He was performing with a troupe at the time and we journeyed to Sharakand to try our luck. The people were most kind and we stayed longer than we had intended. It was an exciting place. My father learnt a lot from their acrobats, who gave most daring displays. And the snake men were truly wondrous!" He shook his head in awe.

"Snake men?" I gasped. "What? Do they slither along the ground with scales and forked tongues?"

"They sound like monsters!" breathed Ellie, eyes wide.

Masou laughed. "They are nothing of the kind!"

he told us. "They are but tumblers with special skills, for they can twist and fold their bodies into incredible shapes. I knew one snake man who could make himself as small as a mouse, or as thin as a veil."

Ellie's mouth dropped open.

"You exaggerate, as usual, Masou," I scoffed.

"A little, maybe," he agreed, "but their feats would astound you. I saw a snake man fold himself into a box you would have thought only a cat could fit in."

"And did you see the Bandy Yasmine when you were there?" asked Ellie.

"It is Banoo Yasmine, O Silly One!" said Masou. "Yes, I did see her." He looked dreamily into the distance. "One day a great shout went up in the village where we were feasting with our hosts. She and her family were coming! Everyone ran to line the path and call greetings and throw petals. And through the village came a slow, stately parade of camels, bearing the noble family and their servants. First in the procession was the king's Chief Minister, the Banoo's father, a very noble-looking man, flanked by guards. His wife and his son rode behind. And then came the Banoo. She smiled kindly on us all as she went by and I believe that the cheer was the loudest for her. She cannot have been more than sixteen, but she was the most beautiful lady I have ever seen."

"Prettier than us?" said Ellie, giving me a wink.

But Masou did not appear to have heard her. He was gazing up to the heavens with a daft look on his face.

"Everyone in the laundry is talking about Bandy Yasmine," said Ellie, licking her fingers to get the last traces of pasty off them. "Mrs. Fadget is in a terrible stew. You should hear her." Ellie sucked in her cheeks and wrinkled her nose till it was just as if the miserable old laundress were there before us.

"Lord preserve us!" Ellie cackled, sounding just like Mrs. Fadget. "What am I to do with all her fancy foreign gowns, which are probably enchanted and will fly away as soon as I try and touch them!"

"That would be a sight," I giggled, "to see her running round the laundry chasing a flock of flying frocks."

"I'd love to set my eyes on that," Ellie went on. "But she'd blame me in the end, as she usually does. She's already told me that the Bandy has a magical ruby and she'll turn me into a black beetle if I do anything wrong!"

"The Banoo would never cast a spell on you,

Ellie," said Masou earnestly, suddenly coming back down to earth. "She is good as well as beautiful."

"I reckon the Bandy has already cast a spell on him!" Ellie whispered to me. "He sounds lovesick."

I tried not to laugh. Now I knew why Masou had made no complaint about tumbling on the cold ground. He was so besotted with Banoo Yasmine that there was no room in his head for anything else.

"Well, ladies," Masou announced, "I cannot stay gossiping with you. I must attend to my practise." He poked his head out of the hedge to make sure there was no one in the herb garden. Then he leaped out, brushed leaves and twigs from his doublet, and carefully straightened his garb. I had to stifle another laugh. I have never known Masou to be so concerned about his appearance. Then he set off with a series of cartwheels.

"I had best be off, too," said Ellie mournfully. "There's a heap of starching to do. Everyone wants their ruff to look the best in front of the new visitors."

She hurried away and I waited a few moments, for it would not look good if we were seen together.

But now I must stop. Lady Sarah is ready at last, and Carmina has just entered our bedchamber, shrieking that the Banoo has arrived!

I am back in my bedchamber again, now getting ready for supper.

When Carmina shrieked, we all rushed from our chamber to join the other Maids at the long windows in the passage, pushing each other to get the first glimpse of our exotic guest. And, after hearing Masou's story, I was eager to see the camels she was sure to bring.

There below us on the waterside rode the four gentlemen of the Court who made up the welcome party. Behind them came a procession of mysterious cloaked and hooded figures. Their cloaks were long and flowing and embroidered with brightly coloured threads. The visitors were riding on Arabian horses and followed by heavily laden carts. But I was sorely disappointed—there wasn't a camel in sight!

"Which one is the Banoo?" asked Penelope.

"I thought the people of Sharakand would be more exotic than this!" declared Lady Jane, looking pleased.

We could see no more, for the procession passed

through the great archway on the waterfront and out of our sight.

"Make haste!" cried Carmina. "To the Glass Gallery. We'll get a good view of the Conduit Court there."

It was lucky that Mrs. Champernowne was not there to see us as we slipped and slid in our stockinged feet along the wooden floors of the Glass Gallery, like eager puppies running for their food. Even Lady Sarah and Lady Jane, who pride themselves on their dignity, were hurrying along—once they had made sure there were no young and handsome courtiers present, of course.

The visitors below were dismounting and handing their horses over to grooms. Palace servants rushed here and there, carrying boxes and chests. One of the cloaked figures stood out from the rest. Her cloak was more magnificent and there was something imposing about the way she moved and the way her companions treated her.

"That must be the Banoo," I said, as Mr. Secretary Cecil and a party of courtiers came out to greet her.

We ran to windows further along the gallery to see if she was as beautiful as we had been told. But no matter where we stood, we were too high to see anything but the top of her cloaked head as she was led inside.

Then I noticed a cart that looked like a cage. "What's that?" I said, pointing. "Could there be an animal in it?" Not a camel, though, I thought sadly. It was too small to house even the smallest of humped creatures.

As we watched, one of the cloaked men strode over, opened the door of the cage, and took hold of a strong, silver chain. We all held our breath as a beautiful black creature, like a giant cat, padded out and gazed regally around the courtyard. I forgot all about camels, and watched in excitement as the creature walked around on the end of its leash, calmly sniffing the air. It looked as royal as Her Majesty herself (if that is not treasonable talk) and I couldn't wait to get a closer look. Not so the palace servants. They all backed away, and one even dropped his burden and ran off screaming.

"What is that beast?" gasped Carmina.

"It is the size of a tiger!" exclaimed Penelope.

"It is probably just an overlarge cat," sniffed Lady Jane, trying not to appear impressed in the least.

"It is so beautiful," I sighed. "Look at its shiny coat! I wonder if Banoo Yasmine would let me stroke it."

"I would not advise you to go near it," said Lady Sarah, "unless you wish to get a close look at its teeth!"

"I wish I knew what it is," I said.

"It is called a panther," said Mary, smiling. "My sister has a tapestry of Noah's Ark, and every time I visit her, my nephew, Thomas, bids me list all the animals. The panthers are his favourite and he chides me if I call them leopards."

"Girls!" came a sharp voice behind us.

We all jumped!

It was Mrs. Champernowne, red in the face and out of breath. "I have been searching everywhere for you. The Queen receives the Banoo soon and not one of her Maids of Honour is in attendance. Come along with you. And look you make deep curtsies when the Banoo arrives," she puffed, as we hurried behind her to the Presence Chamber. "Speak slowly and loudly so she can understand you—and no fidgeting, Grace!"

I might have known that I would be picked out for an extra word of warning. But I only fidget when I get bored. And I certainly wasn't going to be bored with our noble visitor. I wondered if she would bring her panther to the Presence Chamber.

Her Majesty had changed into her lovely gown of

black velvet with a white underskirt to greet her guest. The sleeves are quilted, with slashing to show the white silk underneath, and in each quilted diamond shape rests a tiny gold embroidered leaf. Her ruff is the most exquisite lace and matches her cuffs.

We sank to our knees before the Queen, and then stood chattering nervously as we waited for the Banoo.

"Do you think she'll bring in her panther?" I whispered to Mary Shelton.

"Trust you, Grace," sniffed Lady Jane. "You really are still a child!"

"I hope the panther sharpens its claws on her gown!" I muttered to Mary.

She squeezed my arm. "Take no notice," she said quietly. "We must pity Lady Jane. After all, the Banoo may well draw the eyes of all the young gentlemen, so my Lady Jane is feeling anxious."

Mary was right, of course, but I wasn't as kind as her. I would love to have seen Lady Jane running away from the panther.

Carmina and Penelope had just heard about the Banoo's escape from Sharakand from one of the gentlemen and started to tell us all about it. I had to pretend that this was news to me.

All of a sudden the big doors at the end of the

Presence Chamber swung open. We turned to watch as two large men—with skin as dark as Masou's—strode in and took up their places on either side of the doors. They folded their arms across their chests and looked boldly at us. Their exotic robes sparkled in the candlelight and I noticed that they had long, curling moustaches and beards, quite unlike the men at the English Court. They bowed smartly to the Queen. Then they straightened and stared ahead.

Everyone fell silent as Banoo Yasmine walked in, followed by one Lady-in-Waiting and many servants. She was tall and moved as gracefully as her panther. The Banoo wore a beautiful blue over-robe embroidered with peacock feathers. The elbow-length sleeves were all of a piece with the robe and not laced on like ours. Beneath this, she wore an under-robe of paler blue that fitted closely to her wrists. And there was a decorated leather belt at her waist. Her hair and face were covered with a white silken veil.

As she walked by me, I saw that her under-robe was fastened with tiny blue silk buttons and the belt was set with jewels and silver scrollwork. Just below the waist, the robes flared open to the floor, and to my amazement, I saw that the Banoo did not wear a kirtle but a long loose garment that covered each leg separately. How daring! I admit I would love to try such comfortable-looking hose and be able to walk as freely as a man. If ever I go to Sharakand I will demand to wear a costume like Banoo Yasmine's and sparkly slippers like hers, too, with the curling toes.

"Look at her robes!" Lady Sarah whispered to Lady Jane. I could see they were impressed in spite of themselves.

"They are like gossamer," replied Lady Jane. "I should love a gown in the French style made of such light silk."

"With sleeves of the smoothest satin," murmured Lady Sarah. I imagine she had the design of her own gown in her head already. "I wonder if that shade of blue would complement the copper in my hair," she added, curling a strand of it round a finger, and casting a coy glance at the young gentlemen nearby.

"The bright orange of your hair, you mean!" growled Lady Jane, patting her own blond tresses.

It is a shame that they can only agree for a few moments. But then Mrs. Champernowne frowned at them and they fell silent.

Banoo Yasmine pulled back her veil and sank into a graceful curtsy. Her serving men and women prostrated themselves on the floor in front of the Queen.

Her Majesty extended her hand to be kissed and drew the Banoo to her feet. Now we had a chance to see her face. And Masou was right—Banoo Yasmine was indeed beautiful. Her skin was light brown and she had no lead or rouge on her cheeks. Her eyes were large and dark and outlined with kohl. Her veil covered most of her hair, but I could see that it was black as jet. The women at the Court looked very pale in comparison.

"See how the men are goggling!" I heard Lady Sarah whisper anxiously. "They will flock to her like bees to honey and have no eyes for us."

Lady Sarah was right. All the young courtiers seemed to have lost their wits. They stared at the Banoo transfixed, as if they had been turned to pillars of salt like Lot's wife.

"I warrant she has used unnatural means to enchant them thus," muttered Lady Jane.

"Well, perhaps you could get her to teach you," retorted Lady Sarah, but I do not think her companion heard—or at least she pretended not to.

The Queen was welcoming Banoo Yasmine to England with a fine speech. She has no need to write anything down or practise her words, for they flow from her tongue with ease. I am sure it was a wonderful piece of prose but I had something more important on my mind: where was the panther? Had the Banoo brought it to the Presence Chamber? I tried to peer around her entourage by leaning left, then right. I even stood on my tiptoes but there was no sign of the beautiful black beast. Perhaps it had been left in the stables. I resolved that as soon as I could, I would slip out and discover for myself.

Suddenly Mrs. Champernowne took hold of my sleeve. "I knew you'd fidget, Lady Grace," she whispered. "Now, stand still!"

I think it is most unfair. There's a great deal of difference between fidgeting and looking for a panther!

Her Majesty finished her speech of welcome.

Banoo Yasmine curtsied again to her. "Your Most Gracious Majesty," she said. She spoke in a singsong voice just like Masou. Her English was excellent—there would be no need to speak loudly and slowly to her. "It means everything to me," the Banoo continued, "that you should offer me sanctuary here in your wondrous kingdom." She raised a hand and touched her fingers to her lips. Then she held the hand out, palm up. "Blessings be upon you and your subjects!"

The Queen offered Banoo Yasmine her arm. "I am conscious that you have not the retinue you are used to," she said. "I have therefore instructed Lady Ann Courtenay, Lady Frances Clifford, and Lady Janet Foy and their maids to attend you."

The ladies curtsied and Banoo Yasmine gracefully nodded her head to them.

Her Majesty then addressed us all. "Tomorrow we shall feast and dance. Our fair guest will know that England is a safe haven and that the English Court is her friend." Then she bent her head so only those of us close by heard her next words. "Come with me now to meet my trusted Secretary, Mr. Cecil, and we will discuss the loan you requested."

She led the Banoo away to the other end of the Presence Chamber, where Secretary Cecil stood waiting. The Banoo's guards followed.

The Maids of Honour all curtsied as the Queen passed. Then we gathered together, chattering excitedly.

"Did you see that?" squeaked Carmina. "She's wearing hose! Like a man!"

"And her guards," put in Penelope, "they're so fierce!"

Lady Jane and Lady Sarah began arguing over which gowns they would wear at the feast tomorrow night. I will do my best to avoid the dancing. I am not gifted at it, as I think my partners' toes would agree! But I am excited at the prospect of a feast of welcome—as long as there are not too many speeches—for I know that Mr. Somers and his troupe will surpass themselves in the tumbling display.

I am now perched on the very end of my bed and trying to avoid Lady Sarah's flapping arms! She is ranting at Olwen, her tiring woman, for not having her green damask sleeves ready to be laced on. Fran had Mary and me ready ages ago—but then we do not make a fuss!

Faith, my stomach is rumbling. But no more writing now, for Lady Sarah is ready and we are off to the Great Hall for supper.

In my bedchamber, before dawn

I am writing by the light of a very short candle. It is still dark outside and I have not heard the cock crow. Mary Shelton is still asleep but to my huge surprise, Lady Sarah is already up and gone.

In truth I wager Lady Sarah is already thinking about the feast and dancing tonight. She probably needs at least twelve hours to make ready, if she is to outshine our noble visitor. She will be ordering Olwen out into the cold to find frosty cobwebs and probably sending her back if she does not find the biggest and frostiest. She has a tiny spot on her chin and she says cobwebs are the only remedy.

I am glad I have woken early. It was too late last night to write in my daybooke. After supper the Queen did not need her Maids to attend her, so I went in search of the panther! I was just making my way from the table when Mary Shelton beckoned to me. "Where are you going?" she whispered. "You've only had a piece of ginger tart and four comfits. Are you ill?"

"Not me," I told her. "I am going to find out where the Banoo's panther is. I wager it is kept at the stables."

"I'm coming with you," said Mary, wiping her sugary fingers on a cloth. "Then I can tell my nephew Thomas. He will have eyes as big as cartwheels. But don't go racing off without your cloak. Come, it will take but a moment to visit our chamber first."

It was about nine of the clock when we poked our noses into the stableyard. The lanterns were alight but the shadows were as black as pitch. Holding hands tightly, we made our way across the cobblestones. At the door to the stables we stopped and listened. From inside came some snorts and whinnies.

"I know one thing," said Mary, sounding relieved. "That's definitely horses!"

"What does a panther sound like?" I asked. "Does it miaow?"

"I doubt it," giggled Mary, nervously. "I think it roars like a lion! At least, that's what Thomas told me, but he is just six and has never seen one."

All of a sudden the door opened, making us jump! Then we saw the cheerful face of one of the stable-boys.

"It's only Perkin!" breathed Mary.

"Good even, my ladies," said Perkin, grinning. "I thought I heard voices. But 'tis a deal too late to be riding, I'm thinking. Pray come in out of the cold."

Perkin is my favourite stableboy. He loves the horses in his care and always makes sure that my mare Doucette's coat is gleaming.

"We've not come to ride, Perkin," I told him as we followed him into the dimly lit building. Although I'm not fond of riding, I like the stables. There's a nice warm smell and the horses often stick their noses over their stalls in welcome. "We've come to find the panther," I added. "Is it here?"

"The panther, my lady?" Perkin sounded puzzled. "Is that the name of one of the Arabian horses? They're up at the end there. Fine animals, all of 'em."

"No," I said. "It is the beast that arrived with the Banoo."

"The big black creature, Perkin," explained Mary. "It looks like a large cat."

"Oh, that thing!" laughed Perkin. "So it's called a panther, is it? We thought it were a sort of tiger

31

with no stripes. We wouldn't want it near our horses, with them teeth and claws and growling and suchlike, that much I do know. 'Twould upset them no end." He rubbed the nose of the nearest horse. "And we don't want that, do we, Guinevere?"

The horse snorted softly at him. I looked at the calm row of noses poking over the stalls. Perkin was right. A large cat with fangs would create havoc in here.

"Do you know where the panther is, Perkin?" I persisted. "Surely someone has had to go and attend to it."

He shook his head. "Well, it ain't none of us from the stable, my lady. And we wouldn't want to, neither. They do say it's not an animal at all but an evil sorcerer who takes 'is true shape when darkness falls and wanders about filling folk with the terrors." He held up his lantern and grinned. "Now, let me show you back to the palace, my ladies."

I didn't believe a word of his tale, but we said yes to the lantern because we did not want to trip over in the dark—and for the same reason I held on to Mary Shelton very tightly until we got to our chamber.

Mary is stirring now. It is daylight. I suppose I should get dressed and—

*Afternoon, three of the clock
has just struck*

I had to break off my writing this morning, for there was the most awful screeching outside my chamber. I opened the door to find Lady Jane trying to pull Lady Sarah's ruff off, Lady Sarah slapping back at her, and Mrs. Champernowne trying to pull them apart.

"That is not your ruff, Lady Jane," Mrs. Champernowne was panting. "Yours is in your chamber. Now, get along with you both. I've seen better behaviour from the crows outside!"

Lady Jane hurried off down the corridor and Lady Sarah sailed indignantly into our bedchamber.

I was enjoying the feeling of not being the one in trouble—for about two ticks of the clock.

"And what are you doing, Lady Grace?" asked Mrs. Champernowne. "Standing there gaping, look you. You'll never be ready in time."

It did not take me long to get dressed, and Mary Shelton and I were soon on our way to the Presence Chamber. The palace was bustling. It is always busy at Court but there seemed to be more people than ever.

"It wasn't even this busy at Twelfth Night,"

gasped Mary, as we got entangled in a crowd of carpenters and joiners making their way to the Great Hall with their tools and wood. "I believe they are building something for the revels tonight. I cannot wait!"

I too am excited about tonight and wonder what Mr. Somers has planned for his acrobatic troupe. And I hope I may be able to speak with the Banoo—then I can ask her all about the panther!

After breakfast, Her Majesty was to spend the morning with the Lord Treasurer, dealing with the palace accounts. Unfortunately we were to attend her—all day. Why we have to sit around while the Queen and her minister go on and on about prices of food and furniture I do not know. But it is one of my duties, as Mrs. Champernowne is forever telling me.

We sat on our cushions. Penelope and Carmina began a whispered conversation—which was difficult for them, as they usually like to shriek. On the other hand, Lady Jane and Lady Sarah found it very easy not to talk as they were both sulking magnificently. Mary Shelton had taken up quill and parchment and begun a long letter to her nephew. I guessed it was for young Thomas, for who else would be getting a drawing of a panther?

I sat on my hands for a while. Then I hummed a

line or two of a madrigal about a dying deer until Penelope hissed at me to be quiet. I hadn't got my daybooke so, sadly, I could not write! I could hear sounds of the carpenters in the Great Hall, though I still do not know what they are preparing.

Mrs. Champernowne saw me fidgeting and immediately came over with a basket of tangled tapestry wools. My heart sank at the thought of sorting them.

"Well, Grace," she said solemnly. "You have a choice. You can help me with my wool or you can give Her Majesty's dogs a short walk. A difficult decision, I warrant."

I pretended to think for a minute.

"Oh, get you gone, girl!" she laughed. "If you tarry, I shall have the wool round your hands and you will be a prisoner."

I sometimes forget that Mrs. Champernowne has a kind side. It is usually well hidden beneath her disapproving half! I said thank you and rushed off before she changed her mind.

I took Henri, Philip, and Ivan for a run in the herb garden. I made the walk last for as long as I could. If only I could have met up with Ellie and Masou, but they were far too busy working for tonight's revels. I think I was the only person in the palace who had nothing to do.

It is only just past three of the clock but I suppose I will soon be plagued by Mrs. Champernowne into getting ready for this evening. I could lay out my gown, as I have nothing else to do. It is new and a gift from Her Majesty. I ruined an old kirtle in my duties as Lady Pursuivant and the Queen insisted on replacing it with a fine white silken gown with butterflies embroidered on the false front of the petticoat and Bruges lace edging the partlet.

A few minutes later

I have laid out my kirtle, my sleeves with their laces, my stomacher, my bumroll, my stays, my chemise and partlet, *and* my stockings. Now what shall I do?

Almost midnight, I believe, in my bedchamber

I am in my bedchamber and huddled close to the fire. Although why I am bothering I do not know, for it is giving off so little heat. Fran came in and dampened it some time ago, hinting that I should be better employed trying to get to sleep. Mary Shelton and Lady Sarah are both already in sleep's embrace.

We have had such a night! Soon after the clock

struck five, the other Maids and I processed into the Great Hall. Most of the Court was already there.

"Make sure you carry yourselves well, girls," said Mrs. Champernowne encouragingly as we filed past her. "We do not want the Banoo to think she has come among savages."

Well, I tried to look solemn and stately, but when I saw the decorations I forgot all about it and gasped out loud. You couldn't see the vaulted ceiling for beautiful blue silken drapes—each one painted with exotic birds in flight. The drapes moved in the heat of the candles and it appeared as if the birds were truly hovering above us. The end of the hall was also covered with sweeping drapes, painted with images of camels and their riders. And the whole floor had been laid with golden cloth. It was wonderful.

"This symbolises the desert sands and skies of Sharakand," Mary Shelton whispered to me.

"How do you know that?" I asked.

"Edith told me," she said. "You know Edith, the young seamstress who helps Olwen out now and then? Her sister is married to John Baxter, who works in the forge, and there's a young boy there whose kinsman helped out with the painting."

As I gazed around, I could not help wondering

what had kept the carpenters and joiners so busy all day. There was no sign of their work. But before I had a chance to find out, I realized that everyone had fallen silent and was looking towards the door.

The Banoo stood there with her retinue behind her. Then she glided into the room. She was like the Queen—everyone naturally turned to look at her as she came in.

She seemed more beautiful than ever in a tunic of green satin embroidered all over with golden thread. She was not wearing the strange hose that showed her legs today, but a straight floating skirt under her tunic. Her hair was covered with a golden veil of the finest gauze. But everyone's eyes were drawn to her forehead, for there she wore a circlet of gold cloth, and in the very centre a large ruby hung upon her brow.

Carmina gave me a nudge. "It is the Heart of Kings!" she breathed.

"I never thought we'd get to see it!" gasped Penelope. "Isn't it meant to be magical? It can't be safe to look at it!" She covered her eyes.

"Of course it is," Mary Shelton assured her. "It is just a jewel like any other."

"A deep red jewel!" exclaimed Lady Jane. "Not

everyone could carry that off." She smirked at Lady Sarah. "Certainly not those with red hair!"

"Do you mean Her Majesty?" replied Lady Sarah, looking innocent. "I must go and tell her what you've said." She turned towards the door. "We would not want her to make a fool of herself."

Lady Jane grabbed her arm. "Oh no, Sarah!" she hissed. "Don't, I pray you. It was but a jest. I didn't mean anything by it."

I knew Lady Sarah wouldn't really tell the Queen but it was fun to see the oh-so-superior Lady Jane squirm.

Suddenly there was a deafening fanfare and we all knelt as the Queen entered. Her black and silver gown sparkled with jewels and she wore at least five long strings of pearls. She must have been wearing her largest farthingale, for her skirts billowed out impressively and swished and swayed as she walked. She was magnificent!

The Queen held her hand out to her visitor. "Come, Yasmine. You are our most important guest at this feast. I would have you sit with me at table and tell me tales of ancient Sharakand."

"You do me great honour, Most Noble Majesty," answered the Banoo, in her lovely English.

The Queen led her to a place at her right hand. Secretary Cecil and Her Majesty's Privy Councillors sat on either side. The rest of us took our places at the long tables around.

Servants came to us with bowls of water and cloths and we rinsed our hands, ready to eat. I saw that Banoo Yasmine watched everything the Queen did very closely. Our ways here in England must be very different from what she is used to. For example, I do not believe the people of Sharakand sit at tables. I think they sit cross-legged on beautiful carpets on the floor. And I have heard that some of these carpets are enchanted and can actually fly!

When we had washed our hands, Archbishop Parker, who is currently at Placentia to talk with the Queen of the religious wars in France, began the long prayer.

"All things depend upon Thy providence, O Lord, to receive at Thy hands due sustenance in time convenient. . . ."

I am always thankful to God for my food, but I think it can be said in a sentence instead of a paragraph. While the Archbishop prayed, my mind started to wander. I began to think about where the panther could be. Was it being kept in the armouries? There is plenty of room there. Or possibly the cellars—although I didn't think it would like that unless it enjoys the smell of wine. Then I realised that everyone was chanting the amen and a whole army of servants was approaching with the food.

There were dishes of pheasant, beef, and venison, each one presented first to the Queen and then to the Banoo. Then three young boys staggered in with a great platter on which was balanced a stuffed swan, every feather still in place. I think it is a shame to eat such a beautiful bird, although the only time I came very close to one was at the park of St. James's and it made a horrible hissing noise and chased me round the lake!

Our guest ate very little of the feast.

"Don't they have cows in Sharakand?" I whispered to Carmina as the Banoo pushed some beef around her trencher with her knife. The beef was very tasty, cooked in a prune sauce.

"I have heard they eat awful things like insects and sheep's eyeballs," Carmina told me. I was sure that wasn't true because Masou would have said—and with great relish. But I imagine our food is very different nonetheless. And Banoo Yasmine has lost all her family. I remember I did not care to eat for many days when my dear mother died.

After only two hours, we were hustled away to make the long trek to the Banqueting House, and the tables were cleared for dancing. In the centre of the Banqueting House stood a wonderful marchpane of the Palace of Placentia itself. It had been placed on a trestle table, which was covered in silks and strewn with ivy. The Banoo was delighted with the model. She and the Queen spent ages marvelling over it while the rest of us waited for a helping. Her Majesty insisted on pointing out where we were now and where the Banoo was sleeping and even where Henri's kennel is!

At last it was chopped up. I got a good chunk of one of the towers by the Tilting Yard. I was glad that old King Henry had had them built so tall. I wondered if I could take some for Ellie but I had nowhere to hide it and I dared not spoil my gown by shoving it up a sleeve.

Suddenly a trumpeter blasted a fanfare in my ear and I nearly choked. It was time for the dancing. I would have liked to linger in the Banqueting House and tried a bit of the chapel, but everyone was following the Queen back into the Great Hall so I had to go. The golden sands had been rolled away and benches and chairs had been set around the edge of the hall. The musicians in the gallery were striking up a pavane.

Her Majesty turned to Banoo Yasmine and smiled. "I hope you will indulge my love of dancing."

The Banoo nodded graciously. She did not have any choice, really. Even if she hated the idea she had to agree with the Queen of England!

"Do join us," the Queen continued. "And have no fear that you do not know the steps, for my dear, loyal Christopher Hatton will be your partner, and he is the finest dancer at Court."

Mr. Hatton stepped forwards and offered the Banoo his arm. Her Majesty was being most generous. Mr. Hatton is without doubt the finest dancer at Court and the Queen usually dances with him herself. Then I saw that the Queen was to be partnered by her especial favourite, Sir Robert Dudley, the Earl of Leicester. Perhaps not as generous as I had thought.

"Shall we have this dance, young Lady Grace?" Sir George Tutbury bowed in front of me. It was brave of him to offer. He surely must have heard that it was safer to dance with a donkey than with me! But he was a friend of my father and is always kind to me.

We walked out to join the lines of dancers. The pavane is slow and stately. I am not very stately, but I certainly can be slow! I had to concentrate hard so as not to tread on my partner's feet, but every now and then I looked over to see how the Banoo was faring. Mr. Hatton seemed delighted with his beautiful partner, who was certainly dancing better than me. She must have been practising! The pavane ended and Sir George bowed to me and made his escape. I was pleased to see he was not limping—well, not much.

The musicians now began to play an almain. I was just wondering if I could slip back to the Banqueting House and get some more marchpane, when I noticed Ellie hovering in a doorway. She wasn't meant to be there. I slipped round the dancers to join her, thinking that I would talk loudly about laundry if anyone questioned her presence.

"I came to see Bandy Yasmine. Is that her?" she asked me, pointing at the Banoo, who was making an arch with Mr. Hatton for the others to pass beneath.

"That is *Banoo* Yasmine!" I laughed. "What do you think of her beautiful clothes?"

"I reckon they'd dry easy," Ellie said. Poor Ellie. She works all day and half the night and just sees everything as laundry. "What's that red thing hanging on her brow? It looks like a turnip."

"That is the Heart of Kings," I laughed. "It's her famous ruby."

Ellie quickly put her hand over her mouth. "I didn't say that!" she muttered. "I never called it a turnip!"

"What's the matter?" I asked.

"I'll be cursed," croaked Ellie, glancing round nervously. "I never meant to speak ill of it, did I, Grace? You know that. It's a very beautiful ruby. I don't want no curse!"

"Nothing will happen to you, Ellie!" I assured her. "I think it looks like a turnip, too."

But Ellie turned on her heels and ran off as if a fiend from hell were after her. Poor Ellie, she is so superstitious! It was a good thing she didn't see what happened next or she would indeed have been convinced that she was right. Lady Sarah was just passing by on the arm of her partner. As she did, a servant stumbled right in front of her and dropped the full pitcher of wine he was carrying.

I was certain that Lady Sarah was going to be drenched, but before anyone could move, one of Banoo Yasmine's pages sprang forwards and caught the pitcher in mid-air. And not a drop of wine was spilt! There were gasps of amazement from everyone around, and the page handed the pitcher back to the terrified servant as if nothing had happened. All this took place on the very spot where Ellie had been standing. I decided not to tell her about it. She'd have been certain that the wine was meant to drench her because she had called the Heart of Kings a turnip.

Although Lady Sarah was completely dry and totally unharmed, it seemed that she had to lean heavily on her escort. He did not appear to mind, however, and was most attentive. Then she turned to the page. "I am most grateful to you, sir," she said in a weak voice. "May I know the name of my gallant rescuer?"

The page bowed low before her. "I am Sharokh of Sharakand, O gracious lady," he said, "and ever your humble servant." His accent was like Masou's but much stronger. He gazed at her with large, soulful eyes. I have seen that look many times before. Courtiers are always falling in love with Lady Sarah and staring at her like idiots—it is just the way that Henri stares at his favourite bone. Poor Sharokh! Lady Sarah might enjoy his attentions but she would never consider him as a suitor. He is not highborn enough.

Suddenly there was a loud scraping noise and Lady Sarah was forgotten as we all turned to see what had caused it. The drapes at the end of the hall had been pulled apart and a magnificent wooden tower was appearing, pulled along on squeaky wheels by two of Mr. Somers's troupe. Now I knew what the carpenters and joiners had been up to!

The Queen and the Banoo were already seated where they would have the best view. We hastened to the benches placed round the edges of the hall.

The tower had been painted to look like a turreted castle. The audience gazed upwards as Mr. Will Somers himself appeared at the top. "Gracious Majesty and members of her illustrious Court," he proclaimed, bowing low. "Banoo Yasmine and her most loyal servants, hearken to my tale." Some strange haunting pipe music drifted down from the musicians' gallery. "We take you to the land of Sharakand," Mr. Somers went on, flinging his arms wide to indicate the wondrous scene around us. "A land of enchantment, of golden sands and brilliant sun. A land where camels roam and flocks of bright birds fill the skies. A land where the subjects are loyal and true." With that a curtain opened at the bottom of the tower. "And now I present the men of Sharakand."

Out sprang four tumblers, dressed in long, loose hose and short jerkins to look like men of

Sharakand. They turned somersaults around the floor in a whirl, making the ladies gasp. Then, as a long drum roll began, they leaped into the air and landed with one leg forwards and one leg back as if they'd been split in half. They were all facing the tower, their arms outstretched towards the curtain. And at that a fabulous figure appeared, dressed in a gold silk tunic and long hose. The figure wore a mask, so I had no idea who it was.

"Here before you is the Spirit of Sharakand," cried Mr. Somers. "The noble spirit who strives only for the good of the true king and his subjects."

I guessed this was meant to be the Banoo, but they had named it Spirit, for it would be disrespectful for one of the troupe to represent her in person. The Spirit walked proudly round the hall and the "men of Sharakand" leaped up and followed. They bowed deeply to the Queen and Banoo Yasmine. Then the Spirit came over to where I was sitting. It looked hard at me, which was quite frightening since there was no expression on the masked face. At least it would have been frightening if I had not caught sight of one eye winking at me through the mask. Now I recognised the Spirit of Sharakand—it was Masou!

The Spirit beckoned towards the curtain and out

bounced a little figure on all fours. It was covered in black fur, with painted whiskers, a pair of very perky ears, and a big smile on its face. I recognised this player straight away. It was young Gypsy Pete and he was playing the Banoo's panther. Gypsy Pete has not been with the troupe long. I thought it kind of Mr. Somers to find him a part. And he did it well. He prowled around the floor until he came to the Queen. Then he stretched like a cat with his head bowed down and his bottom in the air. The Queen reached forwards to scratch him between his furry ears and everyone laughed as loud purring noises could be heard. With that the panther bounded to the middle of the floor, sat down, and pretended to clean himself! Masou nudged him with his foot and he immediately sat up and tried to look noble.

It was hard to tear my eyes away from the funny little creature, but now more tumblers were running in through the doors of the Great Hall. They were dressed as soldiers and wore shiny breastplates and helmets.

"The King of Sharakand is cruelly murdered and a new king takes his place," declaimed Will Somers from the top of the tower.

There was a fierce battle between the men of Sharakand and the soldiers. Then the soldiers surrounded the Spirit, who backed away against the tower.

It looked as if it was the end for the Spirit. However, he suddenly ran at one of the soldiers, who was crouched menacingly in front of him. He put one foot lightly on the soldier's knee, the other on his shoulder, and, with an extraordinary backwards somersault, flung himself up at the tower. A moment later he was clinging to the sill of the window, where a soldier immediately appeared with his sword drawn.

But the Spirit was too quick for him. He swung his feet up above his head, knocking the soldier away and landing to stand there in his place. We all clapped. The little panther clapped, too, until he remembered himself and pretended he was scratching his ear.

The Spirit climbed up on to the windowsill, grabbed a trailing ivy, and started climbing towards the very top of the tower. I found my heart was beating fast. The tower was very high and I had never seen Masou do anything like this before. He reached out a hand to pull himself over the parapet, but missed and began to fall! The audience gasped with horror, but we had not seen that he had secretly anchored one foot round the creeper. Instead of crashing to the ground, he hung upside down with his arms outstretched. I knew he was waiting for applause, and he was not disappointed. There was a great burst of clapping as he twisted nimbly upright again and leaped onto the top of the tower.

"But the Spirit of Sharakand is not safe yet!" declared Mr. Somers. "More dangers await!"

Flames were licking their way up the tower! Well, they were really bits of sparkling red cloth, pulled up on thread by someone who must have been hidden on the battlements, but they looked most real. Drums began to beat, faster and faster as the flames grew higher.

The Spirit wailed and wrung his hands in terror.

"It seems that all is lost!" cried Mr. Somers.

But the spirit leaped up to the tower's parapet. He raised his arms high above his head and it looked as if he had grown wings, for he was now wearing a cloak of the most beautiful peacock feathers. Suddenly the drums stopped. I held my breath.

I could scarcely believe what happened next—the Spirit leaped from the tower! For a moment he seemed to fly like a huge bird. And then he was falling. I let out a shriek. Masou was going to be killed. No one could fall from that height and live! And then, just as I thought his brains would be dashed out on the flagstones, he was caught in a golden cloth held by the other members of the troupe. They tossed him back up into the air, where he turned two somersaults and landed on his feet.

For a moment there was a shocked silence. Then the Great Hall erupted with cheers and stamping of feet. Masou ran over and prostrated himself in front of the Banoo and the Queen. I was feeling embarrassed at my terrified shriek, delighted by the Spirit's performance, and very cross with Masou all in one go. This time he has gone too far. He risked his life trying to impress the Banoo and when I see him next I am going to give him a piece of my mind!

Gypsy Pete the panther skidded over and jumped on Masou's back, pretending to lick him. Banoo Yasmine was obviously enchanted with the little panther. Poor Masou! After all his efforts, it was Gypsy Pete who won the Banoo's heart.

In the early hours

I've suddenly realised that the fire is giving no heat at all and I am frozen to the core, so I have come under my bedclothes. I still have much to write about last night, but my fingers are as cold as ice and I fear they will drop off.

After the spectacle of the Spirit of Sharakand, the floor was cleared again and the musicians in the gallery struck up a volta, the Queen's favourite dance. The Banoo was deep in conversation with Lady Catherine so she wasn't dancing. It was lucky for her. When it gets to the bit where your partner lifts you high in the air, he needs to hold on to the bottom of your stays, and I do not think the Banoo had any under her tunic. She may not consider it seemly anyway. I wondered what she must think of our gowns with their low necklines, for she and all her servants are always covered up to the throat—although it does not seem to bother them that they show the shape of their legs!

I noticed that Esther, the Banoo's chief Lady-in-Waiting, was sitting on her own. We had not been formally introduced, but I was dying to learn where the panther was and I was certain she would know—so I slipped over and introduced myself.

And I am so glad that I did! Esther had so much to tell me about Sharakand that I even forgot about the panther. She is so easy to talk to and happy to answer questions. Her English is excellent, though she has always lived in Sharakand. She told me that the Banoo's family have always learned English. It is said that centuries ago the King of Sharakand gave shelter to a lost and wounded English crusader and learnt his language. Since then the monarchs of Sharakand have always welcomed English travellers and the feeling between our two countries has been warm.

There is a myth that the wounded man was Richard the Lionheart himself! It is a wonderful story, but I do not think that the first King Richard would have got himself that lost. And anyway, *he* only spoke French!

"Everyone says the Heart of Kings has special powers," I said. "Is it true?"

"There are many tales," Esther said with a smile, "and some may be true. But the ruby's power must always be used for the good of others."

"So it can't change people into animals?"

"No," laughed Esther. "But it is said that it can cure leprosy if held over the afflicted. And if the sun's rays fall upon it on the first day of planting, then the crops will grow tall and strong."

"Have you seen it work?" I asked.

"It is what we believe," said Esther simply. "And it can resolve conflict. When two people are at odds with each other, they have but to touch the ruby and their argument is laid to rest."

"We could do with that here at Court," I told her, laughing. "Lady Sarah and Lady Jane are always bickering." Though I am sure that even the ruby's magic could not make those two become friends. Then I remembered Ellie's fear. "There are stories that the jewel can put a curse on you."

"It is said to curse only those who would do evil with it," explained Esther. "For those who are righteous, it is a blessing. According to the tradition of our country, a king can only truly become king if

the ruby is wrapped in his headdress at his corona-
tion." She sighed. "Our new ruler is foolish to have
stolen the throne, for the people will not, in their
hearts, believe him to be king without the ruby's
presence."

"Do you hope to return to your homeland one
day?" I asked.

Esther looked sad. "It would not be safe for the
Banoo while that impostor is on the throne," she
replied. "It is my mistress's duty to guard the ruby
well, for one day right will prevail and we *shall* return
to Sharakand." She looked across to where the
Banoo was sitting and her eyes lit up with pride. "It
is a great burden for one so young. But I will always
be with her."

That is just how I feel about the Queen. I would
follow her into exile if I had to, even if it meant
throwing myself off a blazing tower—as long as there
were people at the bottom with a blanket!

At that moment the Banoo herself came towards
us. We both stood and curtsied.

"Banoo Yasmine," said Esther, "this is Lady
Grace Cavendish, youngest Maid of Honour to Her
Majesty."

"I am most happy to know you, Lady Grace,"

Banoo Yasmine said. "But you do not have need to curtsy to me, for are we not equal? Do we not both seek to serve great rulers?"

I was speechless for a moment. I could not believe that the Queen's honoured guest wanted to speak to me as if she were my friend.

The Banoo must have seen my jaw drop, for she laughed. "Come, Grace," she said kindly. "I would have you tell me all about the revels we have seen. Mr. Somers's troupe is most excellent. I am sure we have nothing to better it in Sharakand. Now, who was the dear little boy who played my panther?"

I told her all about Gypsy Pete and how he had joined the troupe last year. I made certain she knew that it was Masou who had taught him his skills. Masou will be pleased with me, I am sure. And talking of Gypsy Pete reminded me of my reason for talking to Esther in the first place. "Where is your beautiful panther?" I blurted out. "I do so want to see it."

"Then you shall," declared Banoo Yasmine. "My Rajah is indeed a fine beast. He stays in my apartments most of the time. But you can come and visit him tomorrow."

So the panther is in the Banoo's rooms—I had not

thought of that. He must be very tame. I cannot wait to see him!

As the Banoo moved her head, the ruby on her brow flashed. And for a moment, I was sure I had seen a star appear in it. I wondered if this was the magic we had heard about.

"Forgive me, Banoo Yasmine," I said, "but your ruby—there was a star—at least, I think so." I suddenly felt a bit foolish. "Mayhap I imagined it."

"No, your eyes have not deceived you," the Banoo assured me. "A star appears in only the most precious of rubies and this one is extremely rare, for the star inside has twelve points, instead of six."

"But how is the star put into the ruby?" I asked.

The Banoo smiled. "It cannot be. It is a wonderful gift of nature. Star rubies are best seen in candlelight. Indeed, they can seem quite dull by day. The twelve-pointed star was said to be the emblem of the Great Karim—the magician who gave the Heart of Kings to my family many centuries ago."

So Penelope was right about the ruby once belonging to a magician. I would have liked to ask more but I did not have the chance, for at that moment the Queen approached with Mr. Cecil and some of her council. I sank into a curtsy with everyone else.

The Queen drew Banoo Yasmine aside to speak

quietly with her. And even though I tried not to listen, I could hardly help hearing that they were speaking of the loan which the Banoo has entreated the Queen to make her.

I had hoped the Queen would agree, since the Banoo finds herself in such unfortunate circumstances. And when the Banoo returned to join Esther and myself she looked so happy that I am certain Her Majesty has done just that. Which means that now Banoo Yasmine can remain in England and, perchance, begin to rebuild her fortune!

I am delighted, but also tired, and though my covers are warm, my fingers are like icicles. Enough for tonight!

Ten of the clock

I have hidden myself away in a window seat in the Long Gallery so that I can write in my daybooke in peace. Something terrible has happened! And my bedchamber is too noisy for me even to think about writing in there, for the other Maids of Honour are all assembled within, still shrieking about the events of the morning.

Straight after breakfast we were all sitting in a small chamber off the Great Hall with some of the young gentlemen of the Court. Carmina was playing the dulcimer and we were all set to practise our French madrigals to sing to the Banoo this evening. Mrs. Champernowne had told us we would not be needed for an hour or so, but we had hardly got to the first chorus of "Cold and Sombre Night" when she was suddenly fussing round us like an old nanny goat.

"Maids, get yourselves to the Presence Chamber straight away!" she bleated. "Her Majesty wants you. No time to pretty yourself, Lady Sarah . . . and no, you may not go back for your knitting, Mary Shelton."

We made haste. No one keeps the Queen waiting. And so we all burst into the Presence Chamber together, almost falling over our feet in our hurry, and curtsied to Her Majesty. We waited for a chiding, for we had rather spoilt our entrance. But the Queen was in good humour.

"My God!" she laughed. "Methinks I see before me a bunch of urchin boys in women's garb!" She looked us up and down. "But stay, young sirs, for you will doubtless make better account of yourselves than my real Maids! Come sit with me—I await the Banoo. She has requested an audience."

We had hardly sat down upon our cushions and were just wondering for what purpose the Banoo had requested such an audience, when the doors of the chamber opened and we had to get up again. There stood Banoo Yasmine, looking most fair in a deep turquoise tunic embroidered with gold petals. She walked forwards and sank into a deep curtsy before the Queen.

"O Gracious Highness," she said. "Most Generous Ruler. In grateful thanks for your endless

bounty, I am come to present to you my surety."
Actually she said a lot more than that, all about the
Queen's kindness in giving sanctuary to a poor humble exile, and all guaranteed to please Her Majesty—
but I cannot remember the rest and probably would
run out of ink if I did. But now we knew why we
were all gathered in the Queen's Presence Chamber,
and I felt a thrill of excitement. As I had suspected,
Her Majesty had agreed to give the Banoo a loan,
and now Banoo Yasmine was come to give her surety
in return. But it is most unusual for any noble to
present a surety in so grand a way. It seemed that
the Banoo had something special in mind!

After the Queen had replied to Banoo Yasmine in
similarly courteous fashion, the Banoo stood and
beckoned to one of her pages.

"Step forward, Babak," she commanded.

Babak was carrying a white velvet cushion. On it
lay a beautiful golden casket engraved with elephants
and serpents. He stepped proudly up to the Queen.

"I offer you the most precious jewel of
Sharakand," said Banoo Yasmine solemnly. She
motioned to Esther, who came forward with a golden
key and unlocked the lid of the casket. We all craned
forwards to see what was inside as the Banoo herself
lifted the lid.

"It is the Heart of Kings!" breathed Lady Jane, who had a better view than the rest of us.

I do not think I have ever seen the Queen so surprised. "My dear," she said, grasping the Banoo's hands in her own, and speaking so low that I could hardly hear her. "Are you sure of this? I would have been well pleased with some other surety. But the Heart of Kings . . ."

"I could offer you nothing less, Your Majesty," said the Banoo. "You have given me new life and new hope. It is only fitting that in return I offer you my greatest treasure. Let those here stand witness this day—there is no greater Queen than Your Most Gracious Majesty, and there is no other to whom I would entrust my precious ruby, the symbol of Sharakand's own true monarchy. Until the true line of kings be restored to my homeland, and my debt to Your Majesty be repaid, the Heart of Kings will lie in the safekeeping of England and her Most Glorious Queen."

For some moments there was silence as we all took in the Banoo's words. Even the Queen seemed awed by Banoo Yasmine's decision. But then she nodded gravely.

"It shall be lodged with the Crown Jewels in the Tower," she told the Banoo. "Be assured it shall rest there safely until such time as it can be returned to you."

"I doubt it not," answered Banoo Yasmine, giving a dignified nod.

"Come then," said the Queen. "We shall speak with Mr. Secretary Cecil and make the arrangements."

The page carrying the casket stepped aside to let them join Mr. Cecil, who was waiting by the window and looking rather dumbstruck at this turn of events. The Maids immediately crowded round to get a closer look at the famous jewel before it was locked away in the White Tower. Lady Jane and Lady Sarah were beside me.

"Don't push," snapped Lady Sarah. "I'm first!"

"Indeed?" replied Lady Jane. "We will see about that!" And she gave Lady Sarah a most unladylike shove. Lady Sarah bumped into me and I fell hard against Babak, the terrified page. The casket flew off the cushion and the ruby was flung out. It traced an arc through the air and then fell to the floor, where it shattered into a thousand pieces.

For the second time the chamber was thrown into a stunned silence—apart from Lady Sarah, who fainted on the spot. The Queen and the Banoo came swiftly over to inspect the damage. I felt sick to my stomach. The Heart of Kings—the most precious jewel of Sharakand—had been destroyed.

The Banoo knelt among the scattered pieces, pale and shaking. The page was staring at the ruby shards, his face ashen.

"I am so sorry!" I wailed. "It was an accident."

I wanted to add that it was not my fault but I did not dare. The Queen was looking furious. I wondered if *I* might be locked in the Tower instead of the ruby!

Slowly, the Banoo picked up a fragment of the jewel. "This cannot be!" she murmured.

"I know not what to say," the Queen responded darkly. "It is unforgivable!"

"No, Your Majesty." The Banoo shook her head. "What I mean is—this cannot be the true Heart of Kings. A ruby would not shatter thus. It is one of the hardest of gems." And with that she fell silent, staring at the pieces of the ruby with a dazed, bewildered look upon her beautiful face.

"Are you *sure* this is not the ruby, my lady?" asked Mr. Secretary Cecil, stepping forward.

For a moment the Banoo seemed not to have heard him. But then she slowly raised her eyes to meet Mr. Secretary Cecil's. "Indeed," she replied at last. "I fear that what we see before us is merely coloured glass." She passed a fragment to him. "See, there are air bubbles such as you may find in glass, but never in a ruby." Her voice shook as she continued. "The Heart of Kings has been stolen!"

A gasp of astonishment went round the chamber. My mind began to race. I could not believe what I was hearing—the Heart of Kings had been stolen and a glass imitation put in its place! I knew I must speak to the Queen as soon as I could and offer my services as her Lady Pursuivant. Until then, I determined to keep my eyes and ears open.

The Banoo was standing now, her hands clasped in front of her. "What am I to do?" she murmured brokenly.

Esther moved forwards to comfort her, but the Banoo straightened her shoulders and turned to the Queen. "I will, of course, find other jewels to offer as my surety, Your Majesty," she said. "But I do not understand how this occurred. The ruby has been locked in its casket in my apartments. I thought it safe, but someone must have taken it during the night."

The Queen was storming up and down in the most foul of tempers. "That such a heinous deed could happen while you are under my protection beggars belief!" she ranted. "I will not have it! If the thief be listening, take warning—give yourself up now, for my anger can only increase and with it my zest for your punishment!"

I found myself looking round the Court to see if anyone was quaking in their shoes. If I had been the thief I would have been on my knees without delay, kissing the hem of Her Majesty's kirtle and begging forgiveness. But no one came forward to confess their guilt.

Her Majesty beckoned to Mr. Hatton. "Get your Gentlemen of the Guard and search the palace. The jewel—and its thief—may still be here. Close the gates. No one is to leave."

Mr. Hatton bowed deeply. "As you command, Your Majesty," he promised. And he swept purposefully from the room.

The Queen's wrath had subsided a little and she turned to the Banoo. "Please do not yet trouble to find other surety. Let my trusty Mr. Hatton and his guards do their job. The Heart of Kings may yet be resting in the Tower very soon."

But I wonder if she really believed it.

Banoo Yasmine asked permission to return to her

apartments. And I saw Esther put a protective arm round her as they slowly made their way to the door.

I was about to step forwards and ask for a private word with Her Majesty—for the sooner I could start my investigations the better. But she must have known what was in my thoughts, for she beckoned to me.

"Lady Grace," she said gravely. "I would remind you that you have . . . new duties to perform for me." She held my gaze for a moment to be sure I had caught her meaning. "See that you waste no time in the execution of them."

I bowed my head. "At once, Your Majesty."

The Queen took my hand. "I know I can depend upon you, Grace," she added in a low voice. "But take care. It may be dangerous."

Once it was seen that the Banoo had left the room, there was uproar. Everyone was in a terrible twitter about what had happened.

"Silence!" roared the Queen. "Get you all gone. And someone clear away this glass, for the very sight of it sickens me."

Mrs. Champernowne chivvied us out and we made our way to our bedchambers.

"What was the Queen talking to you about, Grace?" asked Lady Sarah as we hurried along the passage. "What duties can you do for Her Majesty that we cannot?"

Even at this most serious of times, I could not resist a bit of teasing. "I am sure that Her Majesty would not mind if you did it instead, Lady Sarah," I said sweetly.

"Did what?" asked Lady Jane, who did not want to be left out.

"Walk Her Majesty's dogs, of course," I declared, knowing that this would be the last thing either of those fine ladies would wish to do. "I will fetch their leashes if you will. The dogs must go right up One Tree Hill and across to Duke Humphrey's Tower. 'Tis but a mile or so and only a little icy underfoot. . . ."

But they had vanished and I found I was talking to thin air! And so I went to my bedchamber to write everything down in my daybooke, found the chamber full of shrieking Maids, grabbed my book and penner, and fled!

So here I am, sitting in this window seat, wondering where to begin my investigation.

It occurs to me that the theft must have been well planned, for the villain had a false ruby made and that would take some time. I doubt that any but the Banoo's own servants would have had sufficient time—or knowledge of the jewel—to have such an excellent copy made. It certainly *looked* like the Heart of Kings.

But when had the thief made the substitution? Banoo Yasmine certainly had the real jewel last night, for I saw the Star of Karim in it myself, and *that* could not be counterfeited. So the switch must have taken place during the night. The thief could not easily have left Placentia at once, for he would have been discovered by the guards who patrol the walls after dark. And now that the Queen has ordered that the gates be shut, he will have little chance to flee by day, either. So I believe the thief is likely still at Court.

And I must find him. A small task indeed—there can be little more than two thousand people at Placentia at present!

Back in my bedchamber, late morning

It is very difficult to do any investigating with all the commotion going on and guards stamping about everywhere and Mrs. Champernowne trying to take me off for dancing lessons! But I have made a little progress in spite of it all and must write down my findings. I am sitting on my bed and scribbling as quickly as possible in hope of getting everything down before anyone comes in to disturb me.

As soon as I had finished my last entry I returned to my bedchamber to put my daybooke away and start on my investigation. All the Maids were still there, discussing the theft of the ruby. And I had only just slipped my book under my pillow when Mrs. Champernowne appeared.

"Have you forgotten, girls?" she cried, clapping her hands to get our attention. "Monsieur Danton has been waiting in the Great Hall this past half hour to give you your dancing lesson."

I knew I couldn't gain way with my investigations if I was hopping and slip-stepping so I lurked at the back and, as the others left, I hid behind the door. I thought I had got away with it, when I suddenly heard Mrs. Champernowne's heavy footsteps coming back up the corridor. I darted across the chamber and stuffed myself into the clothes press, on top of a pile of Lady Sarah's shoes. It was terribly cramped! I found myself wishing I could fold myself up like one of the snake men that Masou had told me about.

I had just managed to pull the door to when Mrs. Champernowne came in. "That's strange!" I heard her panting. "I could have sworn on a sixpence that Lady Grace was in here."

Thankfully she did not search any further, but merely sighed and left the room.

I crawled out awkwardly and sat down to consider who would have had access, during the night, to the room where the jewel was kept. The most obvious person, of course, is the Banoo. But it is hard to believe that she is responsible for the theft of her own jewel. She seems to be such a good person—and the Queen herself has shown no signs of doubting her story. Besides, if the Banoo were the thief, she would hardly have drawn attention to the fact that the ruby was a fake!

But, in truth, I realised I knew very little about her. And I would be a poor Lady Pursuivant indeed if I let anyone's winning ways put a fog in front of my eyes. It was possible that the Banoo had tried to trick Her Majesty into thinking she was being given the most precious of jewels. Was Banoo Yasmine intending to take the money from the Queen and never be seen again? If that was her true intention, she must needs be the greatest player in the world to have fooled us all so well. I decided I would have to find out!

I checked that Mrs. Champernowne was not lying in wait and set off—in the opposite direction of the dancing lesson in the Great Hall. I remembered that the Queen had assigned some of her Ladies-in-Waiting to the Banoo during her stay. I hoped to seek out one of their servants and see what they could tell me.

Wherever I went there seemed to be guards, marching here, there, and everywhere, searching rooms for the Heart of Kings. I couldn't find anyone who was serving the Banoo. I decided they must all be in her apartments and I certainly was not going to raise suspicions by questioning them in her presence. I had almost given up when I bumped into Meg Hoggart, Lady Janet's tiring woman. I'd heard that Meg was helping the Banoo with her wardrobe, so I was very surprised to see her coming along the corridor with a huge bowl of raw meat. She bobbed a curtsy when she saw me.

I grabbed the opportunity to talk to her. "Hello, Meg," I said. "Is that for Banoo Yasmine? Do they not cook their meat in Sharakand?"

"'Tis not for the Banoo, Lady Grace," giggled Meg. "It's for that huge black cat creature of hers. Best rump that is."

"Have you seen the panther, then?" I asked eagerly, forgetting for a moment what I was supposed to be finding out.

"Not close up, thank you, my lady," said Meg, backing away to the wall as two guards came through. They gave the meat a suspicious look as they passed.

"That beast is kept in a room on its own," Meg continued. "Thankfully, there's a locked door between it and the Banoo's bedchamber, where I am sleeping, but even so I hardly slept a wink last night, for I could hear it padding around. The Banoo and her women must be used to it, for they never stirred."

"Then you were by the Banoo's side all night," I said. "That's a real honour for you."

"Yes, indeed," said Meg, blushing. "The Banoo favours me, I think, for I am gentle with her fine silks and satins. And I was there, in the dressing room, folding her lovely silken tunic, when Mistress Esther took the ruby off her headdress and locked it in its casket. It makes my blood run cold to think that in the morning, when I followed the Banoo in there and saw her pick up the casket to take to Her Majesty, it wasn't the real ruby inside anymore! Who could have been so cruel as to thieve her precious gem?"

I shook my head, for I had no idea, and Meg hurried off to give the panther his dinner while I made my way straight back to my bedchamber—well, as straight as I could, avoiding guards and dancing masters and Mrs. Champernowne—to write this down.

With Meg at her side all night, Banoo Yasmine had no opportunity to put the false ruby in the casket. Which means the Banoo must be innocent. And I am glad of it!

The Queen's Chambers, the chapel clock has just struck twelve

I am sitting by a roaring fire, writing with one of the Queen's own quills and trying to look ill. But more of that later.

I had just finished writing my last entry when there was a sound in the corridor outside my chamber door. Thinking that Mrs. Champernowne had finally found me out, I was trying to stuff myself into the clothes press again, when I heard a whispered voice outside the door.

"Grace, are you in there?" It was Masou and he sounded worried. "I need to speak to you, Grace!"

I scrambled out and flung the door open. Masou glanced anxiously around him, then darted into the chamber.

"Whatever is the matter?" I asked, knowing that

Masou would not risk coming to my chamber unless it was important. "You look as if you have seen a ghost!"

"It is worse!" he panted. "Something terrible has happened, Grace. Ellie has been arrested by the guards!"

"Ellie?" I cried. "What do you mean, 'arrested'? On what charge?"

"They say she stole the Banoo's ruby!"

"How ridiculous!" I exclaimed. This could soon be put right. "I will go and see Mr. Hatton straight away!" I made for the door. But Masou stopped me.

"You do not understand, Grace," he said. "She had the stolen ruby with her. A guard found it when he searched the laundry basket she was carrying!"

I took Masou by the arms and shook him.

"It cannot be true!" I gasped. "Ellie would never do such a thing." I stared wildly at him. "You cannot believe this of her, Masou!"

"Indeed I do not!" Masou was almost shouting at me. "But the guards believe it, and Her Majesty will believe her guards!"

"What shall we do?" I said, pacing up and down the chamber. I was trembling inside and struggling to keep my wits about me. "Poor Ellie. Do you know where they have taken her?"

"For the moment she is locked in a storeroom by the dairy," Masou told me.

"Then I must go and see her," I declared. "But first I will speak to the Queen. She knows I am investigating the theft. Surely she will see that this is a terrible mistake and allow Ellie to be released while I find the true thief for her."

"I wish I could come with you to see Ellie," said Masou, "but I am wanted by Mr. Somers. I should never have left the practise but I had to let you know the terrible news." He turned at the door. "Be sure to tell her I will solve this mystery," he added, winking at me, "with a little help from the Queen's Lady Pursuivant."

This was just his way of cheering me up. But it did not work. I had a terrible ache of fear in my belly. Ellie taken for a thief! How could this be?

I resolved that when I saw Ellie I would act as cheerful as Masou. And I knew something else that would cheer her up. On my way to the Presence Chamber, I made a detour to the kitchen and begged a bowl of sugared fruits. I didn't mention that they were for the "ruby thief" and I am glad I didn't.

"Of course, Lady Grace!" exclaimed Mistress Berry when I told her what I wanted. "Can't have your ladyship going hungry, can we! You take some manchet bread as well. You never know when you'll be fed, with all that commotion this morning and Her Majesty changing her mind about dinner all the time—though don't go saying I said so, will you, my lady? She is our God-given Queen, after all, and entitled to do as she pleases." She gave me a big piece of bread, still warm from the oven, and half a dozen sugared plums. "What about that Ellie Bunting then? I always thought she had a shifty look about her. You can't trust that type, can you? I was just saying to Jude here . . ."

I thanked her and made my escape. Poor Ellie. The only look she had about her came from hunger and overwork. Would everyone think her guilty straight away? I made for the Presence Chamber. I had to persuade Her Majesty that Ellie could not possibly have stolen the ruby.

The Presence Chamber was as busy as ever and the talk was all about the Heart of Kings. Some were gossiping with great relish about suitable punishments for the thief. I tried not to listen and pushed my way through the throng to the Queen.

Her Majesty was speaking with my lord Robert, the Earl of Leicester. I stood and waited.

"I give you a charge, my lord," the Queen was telling her favourite. "We have need of a diversion for the Banoo and indeed for us all. Something that will help put this sorry business behind us. For we do not want it spread abroad that our Royal Court is not a welcome place."

"I will give it my urgent attention, Your Majesty," he replied.

The Queen lowered her voice. "I have no doubt of it, good Robin."

"Ever your loyal servant, Gracious Majesty," he said with an elegant bow.

My Lord of Leicester can be very high and mighty with the rest of the Court but with Her Majesty he is all gentleness. He thinks the world of her.

The Queen smiled as she waved him away. Then she saw me and summoned me to her so no one could overhear. Her face became grave. "You will have heard what has happened this morning, Grace. It would seem that we do not need the services of our Lady Pursuivant after all," she said. Then she must have noticed the look on my face. "I see you look doubtful. Speak your office," she commanded.

"I am troubled, Your Majesty . . . ," I began.

"How so? Banoo Yasmine has verified that it is the genuine Heart of Kings that has been recovered, and indeed I have seen the Star of Karim in it myself. The jewel is now safely stowed in my ivory cabinet and well guarded in the Privy Chamber. Secret arrangements are under way to have it taken to the Tower." She put her hand on my arm and looked into my eyes. "And the true thief is in custody, is she not?"

"Ellie's not the thief, Your Majesty!" I whispered urgently. "She would no more thieve than she would jump over the moon. And how could she make a false ruby? She is only a poor laundrymaid!"

"Hmm," replied the Queen thoughtfully. "It is a fair point. And I confess I had rather expected the thief to be an ambitious man than a little laundrymaid."

"Then I beg Your Majesty to release Ellie!" I gasped, kneeling in front of her.

"I cannot, Grace," sighed the Queen. "Would you have me release a suspect caught with her illgotten gains? Ellie may have been a pawn in a much larger game. She could have been in someone else's employ. Your loyalty to your friend does you credit, but we cannot be certain she is innocent. Beware that friendship does not blind you."

"I will heed your words, Your Majesty," I agreed. "Everyone must be a suspect."

The Queen stared over my head and spoke—

almost more to herself than to me. "Everyone indeed. Yet I cannot credit that the Banoo has anything to do with this. In my youth, when my sister thought me a traitor, I had to learn whom to trust and whom to fear. And I would swear that Banoo Yasmine speaks truly."

"I am also sure of that, Your Majesty," I assured her. "But I pray that you will give me leave to find the real thief so I may prove Ellie's innocence."

"I will," said the Queen. "But, meanwhile, Ellie Bunting must remain locked up as the thief. It is a great relief to our monarchy that the Heart of Kings, entrusted to us, has been found safe. And yet I would not have the real villain at large in my Court. Therefore I give you leave to continue your search, Grace, but I charge you to act with great care and secrecy. It could be dangerous for you. I do not want to lose a precious goddaughter and I owe it to my good friend, your poor mother, to keep you safe. Tread carefully, my dear."

"Thank you, Your Majesty!" I said. "Nothing shall delay me!" I jumped up, spilling my bread and fruits, and wasted five minutes scrabbling all over the floor to pick them up.

"They're not for me," I muttered. "They're for Ellie. Sugared fruits are her favourite."

I am sure I heard the Queen laugh, but when I looked up she had a perfectly straight face.

I hurried off to see Ellie and told Jonas Beresford, the guard at the door of the storeroom, that I was entitled to visit Ellie as she was my servant. I hoped he didn't know that Ellie wasn't really *my* servant. Luckily for me, he simply opened the door and stood aside to let me in, lighting my way with a candle.

Ellie was crouched in a corner, her head on her knees. She did not even look up.

"Ellie," I called, remembering not to sound too friendly in front of the guard. "On your feet. It is your mistress, Lady Grace."

Ellie got up slowly. Her face was tear-stained and frightened.

"Thank you, Jonas," I said to the guard. "You may go. But leave the candle here. I have need of it."

"Well, I'm not sure I should leave you, my lady," the guard began. "That one there, she's a dangerous miscreant. . . ."

"I have come directly from the Queen herself!" I said haughtily. "I trust you will do as I ask." And indeed I was not lying—I had come from the Queen. She may not have told me I could order the guards about, but Jonas did not know that.

As soon as he had gone, Ellie flew across the room and clutched at my skirts, sobbing. "Oh, Grace!" she wailed. "I never done it. You must believe me."

"Of course I believe you," I said, trying to keep the tears from my own eyes. I pulled her to her feet and hugged her. "I've told Her Majesty that you are not a thief, and I intend to find the real one."

"So I'll be set free?" asked Ellie, with sudden hope.

"Very soon, I'm sure," I told her. "Now look what I've brought you."

I held out the bowl and Ellie wiped her face on her sleeve and ate hungrily. I looked round the miserable little storeroom. It was used to house the masks and other things that Mr. Somers's troupe use in their entertainments. There were wooden trees leaning against the wall, pretend swords and axes, and an enormous dragon's head. I would not like to have been in that room without a candle.

"Mrs. Fadget said I'll never see the light of day again," said Ellie, her mouth full of bread. "She said if the Queen don't leave me in a dungeon to rot, Bandy Yasmine will turn me into a bluebottle—or worse!"

I did not like to remind Ellie what the more likely punishment was for a common thief. I had heard someone say in the Court, not an hour since, that she would likely have her hand cut off and be branded on her cheek with an "F" for "felon."

"Tell me what happened, Ellie," I asked her gently. "How do you think the ruby got into your washing basket?"

Ellie took a sugared plum and bit into it. "I dunno," she said, shaking her head. "The thief must have put it there, I suppose. I was doing my duty, collecting all the dirty linen from the Bandy's servants. There was a whole heap in each room—seems they only wear a shirt for one day and then have it washed! What's wrong with wearing them a week or so like our ladies and gentlemen do? Anyhow, I was on my way down to the laundry when all hell broke loose! There were guards everywhere— and one made a saucy jest about rummaging in my shirts. I laughed, and he lifted the linen in the basket, and . . . and . . ." Tears began to run down Ellie's face. ". . . He found the jewel!" she sobbed. "But I never put it there!"

"Of course you didn't, Ellie," I said soothingly. "I know you would never do such a thing. And we can easily prove it."

"How, Grace?" gulped Ellie.

"It is easy," I said with a smile. "We just have to

show everyone that you didn't go anywhere near the dressing room, so you can't have taken the ruby. There was a guard at the door who would have seen you go in!"

"But I *did* go in the dressing room!" howled Ellie.

My heart sank. For a brief moment I had thought that Ellie's nightmare was over.

"Are you sure?" I asked in desperation.

"Yes," answered Ellie. "When I arrived to ask for the Bandy's linen, that Mistress Esther woman told me they wanted a wine stain taken out of those funny hose things the Bandy wears. They was ever so busy, so she said I was to go into the dressing room and fetch it meself."

"Did anyone see you go in?" I asked.

Ellie nodded. "The dressing room door had one of Mr. Hatton's men guarding it, but there was no one in the room itself. I saw a casket on a table. It was beautiful, with golden oliphants and other strange things round it. But I never touched it—or anything but the hose—and I never even *saw* the ruby. And I wouldn't touch it if I had—what with it being cursed and all."

So Ellie had had the opportunity to take the ruby! She could even describe the very casket it was in! I realised it was going to be very difficult to prove her innocence. Then I remembered that Esther had used a key to open the casket this morning and I saw a glimmer of hope.

"The casket was locked when it was taken to the Queen this morning," I said excitedly. "So surely it was locked when you saw it—which means you couldn't have taken the Heart of Kings." I gave her another hug. "Try not to worry. I will find the real thief."

"You be careful," said Ellie. "Mayhap Banoo Yasmine used her dark arts to steal her own jewel."

"I don't think so," I told her. "But it must have been someone who had access to her dressing room. I shall go to the Banoo's chambers straight away."

"Don't forget, the ruby will curse wrongdoers, Grace," said Ellie earnestly, as I left. "Be sure to look out for anyone who has turned green, or whose nose has dropped off or something!"

I made my way to the Banoo's apartments, thinking I would say I had come to see Rajah, the panther. After all, I had had my invitation the night before. As I went up the tower stairs, I met Mary Shelton.

"You did well to avoid dancing practise," she said with a smile. "Monsieur Danton was in a terrible mood. We couldn't do anything to please him. Where are you off to now?"

"To the Banoo's apartments," I told her. "I couldn't wait any longer to see the panther."

Mary's eyes lit up. "Let me come with you," she said. "Then I can tell Thomas all about it."

Samuel Twyer, one of Mr. Hatton's guards, stood outside the Banoo's chambers. He recognised us as Maids of Honour and stood aside to let us in.

The Banoo had been assigned rooms that looked out over the Conduit Court. There was one long chamber for receiving guests with three doors leading from it. The middle one stood ajar and I could see that it led to the bedchamber, but the other two were closed. The walls of the chamber in which we stood had been hung with tapestries and the floor strewn with deep carpets. I had heard of carpets like this, but it felt very strange to walk on them, quite unlike rushes. I didn't think I would like carpets in my chamber. I love it when Fran has strewn fresh rushes and herbs on the floor. It smells so sweet. But Her Majesty must have made sure that the Banoo had familiar things about her, for she had been forced to leave so much behind when she fled Sharakand. That was kind of the Queen, I thought. The Banoo's two guards stood, statue-like, by the window.

To our surprise, Banoo Yasmine had her arms

around Esther, who was sobbing. Her other servants stood around watching in dismay.

"You witness my disgrace," Esther cried when she saw us, "for it is all my fault that the precious Heart of Kings was stolen! Its safe return does little to ease my guilt."

"Calm yourself, my dear Esther," said Banoo Yasmine.

"But I left the casket unlocked!" wailed Esther. "Last night after the feast and revels I was very tired. I put the jewel away hurriedly and I must have forgotten to lock it. As soon as I came to collect it this morning I discovered my error. Imagine my relief when I saw that the jewel was still safe inside. But it wasn't the real ruby. I ought to have looked more closely. You should banish me from your sight, my lady."

"Enough!" said the Banoo soothingly. "Why should I want to lose my dearest friend? And the matter is over. The jewel has been found and the thief apprehended."

So the casket had not been locked. This was terrible news for Ellie.

"Forgive me, Banoo Yasmine," I said, "but are you certain that Ellie the laundrymaid is the thief?"

The Banoo and Esther both stared at me in astonishment.

"The jewel was found in her basket," replied Esther. "And no one else was let into the dressing room after the ruby was put away last night. The room was guarded at all times because the Heart of Kings was in there."

I looked at Esther thoughtfully, wondering if she could have taken the ruby. But, unfortunately, I had to acknowledge that it was unlikely. For one thing, I believe her to be completely loyal to the Banoo, and her horror at the theft seemed real enough. And for another, Esther would have spent the night in the Banoo's bedchamber. If she had risen to go and steal the ruby from the dressing room, poor, sleepless Meg would have been sure to notice. And Meg told me only this morning that none of the other ladies were disturbed in the night, so Esther cannot be the thief.

But this was not helping Ellie one jot and I realised I could not ask any more questions, for I have to keep my investigations secret.

At that moment a page came in with a letter for his mistress. I recognised him. He was the one who had saved Lady Sarah from a drenching last night. He glanced at us and I think he was actually disappointed that she wasn't with us.

"Thank you, Sharokh," said the Banoo.

He gave a deep bow and was about to take his leave when the door to the chamber opened again and in came another page. He had Rajah the panther with him! I gasped with delight as Rajah padded regally into the chamber, his black coat gleaming like polished ebony in the candlelight. He spotted Sharokh and immediately began to pull on his leash like an eager puppy after a favourite toy. Rajah was clearly keen to go and see the page, but Sharokh backed away swiftly with a look of utter panic on his face. I was surprised to see this because all the other servants of the Banoo seem entirely comfortable with the panther. I had thought that only the English were nervous of the big cat, but Sharokh was obviously terrified.

"Take Rajah to the other side of the chamber, Anoosh," ordered the Banoo, smiling. With great difficulty, the young man pulled the panther over to the window. Sharokh immediately ran for the door and disappeared, without even stopping to bow!

"Rajah adores Sharokh and wishes only to play with him," explained the Banoo, laughing. "But Sharokh is in terror of him. I have never understood why, for Rajah is as harmless as a kitten." She walked over and stroked the panther, which rubbed his head against her happily. "Rajah is my dear friend. He and Esther are the nearest I have to kin now. I expect you ladies are longing to pet him."

I was!

"Come forward slowly and show no fear," the Banoo instructed.

I did as she said. I could feel my heart thumping in my chest with excitement. I touched the panther on his silky black head and he immediately rolled over onto his back! Banoo Yasmine stroked his belly and I did the same. He felt soft and warm like one of the kitchen cats. Then he rolled over again and began to pull at the tassel of a cushion.

"He is young and loves to play," said the Banoo. She pulled the tassel out of his reach. "You must not toy with Her Majesty's property!" she told him. "See, here is your ball." She produced a small ball made of strips of leather. Rajah batted it and then rolled over again with his paws in the air.

"Come and pet him, Mary," I urged, reaching out to stroke his belly once more.

But Mary could not be persuaded to come any closer to the panther. "I can see all I need from here," she said nervously. "I have more than enough to tell my little nephew."

"Panthers are usually wild and untameable creatures," Banoo Yasmine said, smiling at Mary. "But I have had Rajah since he was a cub. I hand-reared him myself and he is very well-behaved."

Mary still looked ill at ease, so I decided it was time we took our leave. And in truth, I was feeling guilty for having fun while poor Ellie is locked up in a storeroom.

Outside the apartments I stopped to speak to Samuel Twyer. I thought I would play the silly maid and find out what I could. I have watched Lady Sarah and Lady Jane do it often enough in order to gain some favour from a young courtier.

"Tell me," I breathed, pretending to be avid for gossip. "Who was guarding the jewel through the night when it was stolen? Has he been taken from his duties? He is surely in great trouble with Her Majesty. And, indeed, are any of us safe in our beds?"

Mary looked at me as if I were mad, but the guard smiled.

"No cause for alarm, my lady," he said. "It was Harry Thornham on duty all last night and he's a true and honest gentleman. Harry says no one went in that room until the thieving little maid this morning, not even Banoo Yasmine. And you can sleep safe, my lady, for we'll make sure any miscreants are quickly apprehended."

"Thank you, Samuel," I said, fanning my face with my hand. "You have quite relieved my mind." He had not, of course. Quite the opposite, in truth, for it still seemed that only Ellie could be the thief!

I was lost in thought as we made our way down the tower stairs—when suddenly I realised that Mary was talking to me.

"Grace!" she frowned. "You haven't been listening to a word I have said! Whatever were you doing playing the silly maid with that guard? It is not like you at all." Then she stopped and stared at me. I tried to look innocent but obviously didn't manage it. "Of course," she said, smiling. "I should have known. You were play-acting! You are determined to free Ellie, aren't you? Though how I cannot imagine."

"Nor can I, Mary," I said sadly. "For everyone's finger points to her. But there must be a way of finding the real thief, for I know it is not Ellie." And, with that, I returned to my thoughts, wondering what I could possibly do to further my investigation and free my friend!

We were on our way back to our chamber when we met Mrs. Champernowne bustling along the corridor. I waited for her to chide me over my missed dancing lesson but she turned to Mary instead.

"Look lively, Mary Shelton," she said. "The Queen has invited Banoo Yasmine and her party to go hunting in Greenwich Park. She hopes to lift her guest's spirits."

So this is what my Lord the Earl of Leicester had organised. I should have guessed it would involve horses, for both the Queen and the Earl are superb riders and can easily outstrip the rest of the Court. This would give the Queen's favourite an opportunity to have her to himself. I do not think he had thought overmuch about cheering up the Banoo! I confess my heart sank at the thought of hunting. I am not a good rider and I hate to see the deer killed. Besides, I had no time to be galloping about Greenwich Park when Ellie needed my help. I had just resolved to look weak and ask to be excused when Mrs. Champernowne turned to me.

"Her Majesty seems to think that you will not be well enough to accompany us, Grace," she said, puckering her mouth as if she had sucked on a lemon. "I must suppose that that is also why you did not come to the dancing practise."

Mary looked as if she wanted to laugh and I had to turn my head for fear she would set me off giggling. "Whatever Her Majesty wishes," I replied, trying to sound feeble. "I am so disappointed. There is nothing I would have loved better than the hunt—but I dare not disobey."

"Humph!" snorted Mrs. Champernowne. "Then get you to Her Majesty's Privy Chamber. There is a roaring fire there."

"I will," I croaked. "But, dear Mrs. Champernowne, I have a fancy to write down my meditations. I will just fetch my daybooke from my chamber first."

Mrs. Champernowne stomped off to ready herself for the hunt, for she will be of the party even though she will not ride.

I could not believe my good fortune! The Queen was giving me a wonderful chance to investigate while everyone was away from the palace. For a moment I felt quite cheered up—until I remembered that I have made no progress at all and, worse, have no idea what to do next.

So now here I am, sitting by the fire. My writing is a little strange, for I forgot to collect my penner. I have used one of the Queen's quills, but I did not dare trim it to suit my hand, so the result is a little wobbly. Luckily I will be finished with the quill in a line or two, for I have written all I can while I wait for the Court to go off to the hunt. As soon as they are gone I will do some hunting of my own.

I am sitting in an alcove with a fine view over the Cellar Court. It is dark outside, but her Majesty loves to show off the palace where she was born, so all the courtyards have been lit each night since our visitors arrived. They look quite magical with little candles under all the hedges.

Everyone has returned from the hunt and is getting ready for supper, so I have time to write.

As soon as I heard the blast of the hunting horn and the sound of the hooves galloping away into the distance, I ran to my chamber and hid my daybooke at the bottom of my chest.

Next I went to the kitchens. It wasn't part of my investigation—I was starving! Everyone else was to be fed at the hunt and I had been forgotten. The kitchen workers and the other servants were all sitting round the big table in the middle of the Great Kitchen just finishing their dinner. Mistress Berry stood and curtsied as she saw me.

"Lord love us, Lady Grace!" she exclaimed when I begged her for some food. "I thought all the Court had gone! Let's see what I can give you—for all the fine food has been packed on the carts and taken off to the hunt." She scurried off and soon came back with two apples and a piece of cheese. "Will this do for now, my lady?" she asked anxiously.

I had to say yes, although I would have preferred a bit of leftover veal pie like the one I could see disappearing down the scullion boy's throat.

I made quick work of the cheese and apples as I headed for the Banoo's apartments. I had decided to examine her dressing room. Somehow, someone other than Ellie had got in there without being seen and I was determined to find out how.

"Where are you off to, Grace?" said a voice behind me. It was Masou. He ran up and placed a hand on my brow. "There must be something wrong with you if you are not out with the Court." He grinned. "For I know how much you love to hunt!"

"But I *am* on a hunt," I told him. "And you can help me instead of making silly jokes."

"At your service, my lady," Masou said with an elegant bow. "Anything that will help free Ellie."

"We are going to the Banoo's rooms to find out how the thief stole the jewel without being seen."

"Then I am doubly at your service!" Masou was in the middle of another ridiculous bow, when he suddenly stood up straight. "But I cannot present myself there like this," he cried. "I must put on finer clothes for that great lady."

I grinned. I had forgotten that Masou was love-struck. "God's Odkins, Masou!" I exclaimed. "The beauteous Banoo has gone with the hunt. She will not be there. Nor will anyone else, I hope."

We climbed the stairs to the apartments.

Samuel Twyer was still there, guarding the outer door. He stood to attention as we approached. "I beg your pardon, my lady," he said, "but no one is to enter until the Banoo returns."

"Is there no one in there who could allow us entry?" I asked, disappointed. I tried to flutter my eyelashes at Samuel but probably just looked as if I had a twitch.

"There's no one but that big cat, my lady," answered Samuel, "and I do not intend to ask him!"

"'Tis a pity," said Masou, "for Lady Grace and I have a wager, do we not?"

"Do we?" I asked.

Masou glared at me.

"Oh, indeed . . . that wager!" I mumbled, realising that Masou was up to something.

The guard looked interested. It seems that no gentleman can resist a wager. It was clever of Masou to think of it—though I was not going to tell him that. His head is quite big enough.

"What may that be then?" Samuel asked me.

"It's . . . well . . . ," I faltered. "Um, tell Mr. Twyer about our wager, Masou."

Masou's eyes twinkled. "I am of the opinion that a simple laundrymaid is not clever enough to think of stealing the Heart of Kings. It is my belief that it could only have been done by magic," he told the guard. "But my lady here tells me that I speak nonsense and will pay me nothing until I can show her the signs."

"There's no magic here," said Samuel firmly. "We have our thief. So I'd be keen to join that wager—if I had coin enough."

The Gentlemen of the Guard are often younger sons of noble families, so they have no chance of inheritance and are always in need of money. I pulled some silver coins from the purse on my belt and put them in his hand. "I will stand your wager," I told him, "for we are both on the same side in this matter."

Samuel stood aside, looking fixedly down the corridor so he would not see us go in. Masou opened the door and we both slipped quickly through it.

As Samuel had said, there was no one in the long chamber where the Banoo received her guests. We looked at the three closed doors that led to her privy rooms.

"The one in the middle is her bedchamber," I said.

"So that leaves two doors," responded Masou. "One on the right and one on the left. And we must choose carefully, for behind one lies the panther with his sharp teeth and claws!"

I smiled. "Rajah is not fierce," I told him, as I slowly opened the door on the right and peeped inside. "In fact, look, he's sleeping like a baby."

Rajah heard our voices and lifted his head. Masou stepped back quickly. But Rajah merely looked at us sleepily, gave a great yawn, and laid his head down again.

"He's a big baby," said Masou.

I shut Rajah's door softly and we moved to the other. Masou opened it and we peered inside. The chamber was just like any other dressing room—full of clothes, trunks, presses, and chests. It was all lit faintly by the wintry light coming in through the window.

"The window provides another way of entering

this chamber," I pointed out. "The thief could have sneaked in that way and no one guarding outside the door would have known." I went over to it and opened the casement. Masou and I leant out. We could see our breath in the cold air. I looked down to the flagstones of the Great Courtyard, far below. "Is it possible to climb up here from the ground, do you think?" I asked Masou. "We're ever so high."

Masou shook his head. "Only a spider could make that journey," he replied. "The bricks are too smooth to offer hand or footholds, and there are no window ledges."

I sighed. "So the thief could not have come in this way."

"Wait a minute!" cried Masou. He was craning his neck to try and see the top of the tower. Then, to my astonishment, he leaped up onto the windowsill!

"Whatever are you doing?" I cried.

"It may not be possible to climb *up* to this window," he said, holding the window frame as he leant out. "But someone might have climbed *down* from that casement above. See, this brickwork is more decorated. I can put my hand here and my foot thus and . . ."

And with that he had gone!

I hardly dared to look. He balanced his feet on tiny ledges of brick and clung with his fingertips to ridges barely visible above him. Then, before I knew it, he had swung up like a monkey and was perched on the ledge of the window above. All I could see were his legs dangling down, and above, the grey clouds scudding across the sky. I felt as if the tower were falling onto me. It made me feel quite sick.

"It is a room with many palliasses in it," Masou called down to me. "I wonder who sleeps here. I shall enter." There was a pause. "Or at least, I would if the window had an opening!"

Then he called again. "Wait! There is another window to this chamber—a smaller one. I am certain I can reach it."

"Be careful!" I shouted.

Masou stretched out his hands and I thought he would plummet to his death. I covered my eyes. What a coward you are, Grace, I thought, and opened them again. Masou was clinging by the tips of his fingers to the ledge of the other window. Then he pulled himself up and I heard a curse. "By Shaitan!" he cried. "I can open this one but it is far too small for me to go through. Move away. I am coming back."

It seemed we were doomed to failure. I stepped

back into the dressing room and Masou swung in through the window and dropped lightly onto the floor. Together we scoured the room for any other possible entrances or exits. But there was nothing.

"So we are back to magic then!" I groaned. "It is a shame we didn't have that wager, Masou, or you would have won some money. Poor Ellie."

"I tried to visit her this morning," said Masou, "but they would not let a humble tumbler past the guard."

"Then we shall go together," I decided. "They will not deny you if you are with me."

As we left, I pressed some more coins into Samuel's hand and told him that there was no sign of magic and he had won his wager.

Then I smiled—coyly, I like to think. "I pray you will not tell anyone that we were here, Samuel," I said winningly. "I would not want Banoo Yasmine to learn that we were dealing lightly with a matter that means much to her."

"I don't know what you're talking about, my lady," said Samuel, grinning. "No one has passed through this door since the Banoo herself left to go hunting."

Ellie's face lit up when she saw us. "What did the Queen say when you told her the casket was locked and I couldn't have stolen the jewel?" she asked eagerly. Poor Ellie was trusting that I had already cleared her name.

"I am sorry," I said, trying to make myself comfortable on a rickety painted box. "But the casket had been left unlocked. So I could prove nothing."

Ellie's face fell. "I might have known it were too good to be true," she murmured. The candle spluttered suddenly. "Oh no," she whispered. "That flame won't last long. And now it looks as if I'll be needing another light."

"I will see to it," I told her. "Don't you worry. Now, Masou and I have been up to the Banoo's chambers," I went on, trying to sound cheerful. "We thought the thief might have used the window to enter."

"I never thought of that!" said Ellie. Then she frowned. "Though it's too high up, surely. He would have to fly in like a bird!"

"Masou has proved that it is possible for a skilled tumbler to climb down from a window above," I explained.

"So you only have to tell Her Majesty and I'll be free," Ellie declared, her face lighting up again with sudden hope.

"There is just one problem," said Masou solemnly. "The window above is not large enough for anyone to climb through. I doubt even Gypsy Pete could make himself so small."

Ellie sighed heavily. "I got my hopes up again," she whispered. "I truly am cursed by the ruby."

"We have not given up, Ellie," I told her.

There was silence. None of us seemed to know what to say next. Then Masou came to the rescue.

He leaped up and addressed the dragon's head in the corner. "Ah-ha!" he declared. "I see an old foe! I thought I had slain thee, foul worm, last St. George's day." He picked up a wooden sword and capered about, parrying and thrusting at the beast, much to Ellie's delight.

"I remember that feast," I said, grateful to Masou for giving Ellie back her smile. "You should have seen it, Ellie. Masou slew the dragon and everybody cheered as he carried the maiden to safety."

"It near broke my back!" said Masou ruefully. "That was French Louis under that veil."

"I know," I giggled. "I could see his beard!"

"Show me how you fought the dragon again, Masou," pleaded Ellie.

And Masou capered around the tiny storeroom, brandishing his sword, while Ellie clapped her hands, happy for a moment.

"You are a good audience, Ellie." Masou grinned. "I wish you had been there when I scaled the tower just now. Grace seemed remarkably unimpressed. Rather than applause, I heard only squeaks of fear from my lady! *You* would have cheered me on." He sighed. "If I could just have squeezed myself through that little window."

We were all silent. The hopelessness of Ellie's situation seemed to hang over us again like a dark cloud.

Then Ellie suddenly threw her arms in the air. "That's it!" she cried.

We looked at her in astonishment.

"You may not be able to fit through the small window, Masou, but one of them snake men could. You remember, you told us about them."

"By my hat!" exclaimed Masou in surprise. "I had not thought of that!"

"Is it possible, Masou?" I asked. I could not bear to give Ellie any more false hope. "Do you think a snake man could get through that window?"

Masou frowned. "Indeed," he said thoughtfully. "I am certain that a snake man such as those I saw in Sharakand could do it."

"Then that could be our answer!" I declared, and found I was gripping the sides of my seat hard with excitement.

"But, alas, there are no snake men in Mr. Somers's troupe," sighed Masou. "And in truth, I have not seen nor heard of one in all my time in England."

"But there could be one among the Banoo's servants!" I almost shouted.

Masou's eyes lit up and he nodded.

"Well done, Ellie!" I said, jumping up and hugging her. "You have found the answer!"

"Now we just need to find the snake man!" put in Masou with a grin.

"It can only be one who is sleeping in that chamber above," I pointed out. "For only one of them would have easy access to the window, and could slip out in the night without rousing the others. Can you find out who is sleeping in there, Masou?" I asked eagerly.

"Without delay!" he promised.

And though we had to leave Ellie, we were leaving her with some real hope this time—and a candle that I insisted the guard give her.

From my hiding place in the alcove I can hear the other Maids coming along the passage on their way to supper. How hungry I am! The cheese and apples were days ago—or so my stomach seems to think.

Late morning

I have come up to the musicians' gallery in the
Great Hall to write, as I will not be disturbed here,
with luck.

As I was leaving the Great Hall after breakfast,
Masou hissed at me from behind a door. I joined
him and he told me that he had discovered who is
sleeping in the room above the Banoo's. It is three of
her pages: Anoosh, Faruk, and Babak. Surely one of
these must be the thief!

And I have made a plan to find out which one.

First I thought about the three pages. Two are
young and thin. Either could be a snake man. The
third one, Babak, who presented the ruby to the
Queen, is very different. He is plump and even older
than the Queen. He is far too old and fat to be

clambering about on the palace walls and squeezing himself through tiny windows. But I thought his age might be of use to me because he could have years of knowledge of the Banoo's retinue. So, I decided to find him first.

After a long search I came across him taking some empty bowls back to the kitchen. I think Rajah's breakfast had been in them, for they had been licked clean. I am very pleased with the excuse I thought of to speak with him.

"Noble sir," I said. "I would beg a few moments of your time, for I seek information and I believe you are the only person who can help me."

He was flattered, I could see. "At your service, gracious lady," he said, making me a bow with a great flourish. His English was very heavily accented and he rolled his "r"s like the purring of a cat.

"There has been word of a potential betrothal between one of the Banoo's pages and Lady Sarah Bartelmy," I told him in a low voice. "It is but a whisper, and we know not which young man it concerns, but the Queen would like to learn a little more about Anoosh and Faruk. Of course, she cannot ask directly, if you catch my meaning. But you are well acquainted with them, I think."

"I serve the Banoo's family all my life," said Babak, puffing out his ample chest. "I see her grow from baby to beautiful woman. But Anoosh and Farrruk—they are newly come into her service. I know little of them."

"Are they of good birth at least?" I asked. "I know the Queen would not countenance a suitor for Lady Sarah who was from a family of say . . . tumblers!"

Babak smiled. "They are both silly young men, as most young men are. I am thinking your Queen would not like a match between a Maid of Honour and one of them, no matter what family he is from."

"Ah, yes, family," I said, in a desperate attempt to bring him back to the point. "Do you know their families at all? Are they of noble birth, do you think?"

Babak smiled broadly. "I do not know," he said, shaking his head. "I would not have thought so. But who can tell with foolish young men? They talk always of horses or games or young ladies—not of family or childhood. Indeed, they are all but children still."

"Horses," I said, trying to get any information from Babak that I could. "You said they talk of horses. Do they like to ride? Are they especially skilled at riding?"

Babak shrugged. "They can both ride, of course. I do not know if either is very expert. I am sorry I cannot be of more help to your Queen."

I realised that I was wasting time asking Babak about Anoosh and Faruk. He clearly did not know enough about either of them to help me. I said goodbye and hurried away, hoping that he would never mention our conversation to the Queen, for I have used both her and Lady Sarah shamefully.

I racked my brains, trying to work out how I could learn whether either Anoosh or Faruk was the thief. I knew that in order for the thief to enter the chamber where the ruby was kept—without being seen—he could only have entered by the window. That meant he had to be an accomplished climber or tumbler, like Masou. And, since the only way to reach the window was by climbing out through the tiny casement of the room above, the thief must also be a snake man of remarkable ability. Surely there was some way to find out whether Anoosh or Faruk possessed these unusual acrobatic skills.

The palace was very busy, as ever, and it was hard to put my mind to the problem, so I got my cloak and collected the Queen's dogs. It was a bright morning and I felt sure the cold air would clear my head.

As Henri, Philip, and Ivan rushed up and down the Tilting Yard, fetching sticks, I tried to devise a plan for testing the pages. At last I thought I had the perfect scheme. I would claim that the door to their bedchamber was shut fast and if they wished to sleep in their beds tonight they would have to climb the walls and slip in through the window. But how should I approach the matter? If it was clumsily put, the thief would know straight away what I suspected. I needed expert help, and I knew where to find it.

I think Mr. Somers was rather surprised when a Maid of Honour, with three yapping dogs, turned up at tumbling practise asking for Masou. He was too courteous to argue, and politely agreed that the Queen's dogs would benefit from having an expert tumbler like Masou to teach them to beg. Looking rather puzzled, he bade Masou go with me.

Once we were back out in the Tilting Yard I told Masou my plan.

I had to wait a long while until he had finished laughing.

"You have given me much joy," he chortled. "Your plan is as good as one of Paul the Dwarf's jokes—that is to say, terrible! If either Anoosh or

Faruk is the thief, he will know what you are about straight away—and if not, he will think you have lost your wits!"

"Well then, Mr. Clever," I asked, "how would *you* test someone's tumbling skills?"

Masou said nothing. He simply walked forwards and pretended to trip over an astonished Ivan. However, instead of falling flat on his face, he turned the trip into a forward roll and stood up again, unhurt.

"It is simple," he told me. "You cause them to fall over and see what they do. If they are tumblers, they will turn it to their advantage."

"But you knew you were going to trip," I protested. "Surely even an expert tumbler will fall if taken by surprise."

"Impossible," said Masou with a grin. "It is in the blood. And whoever climbed into the Banoo's dressing room must be truly skilled in these things."

"Very well." I shrugged. "I will attempt to trip up Anoosh and Faruk and see what they do."

All of a sudden, Masou crouched down on his haunches in front of Philip, held his hands out in front of him, and began to pant. Philip jumped up and licked his face. I had no idea what was going on. Was this a different test he wanted me to do? I wondered.

"Methinks you should find another to teach the dogs, Lady Grace," came a voice. "Masou is more like to be chewed than be a tutor." It was Mr. Somers! Masou must have seen him approaching and remembered what he was supposed to be doing.

"Come, lad," said his master merrily, "for we have not the top point of our pyramid until you arrive."

It still makes me chuckle to think of the troupe solemnly balanced on each other's shoulders, waiting for Masou.

Now it is well past noon and almost time for dinner so I will put my daybooke and penner back in my chamber. Then after my stomach is full I will go and find the unsuspecting pages and see how well they trip!

Bedtime, in my chamber

I am first to retire. I want to write in my daybooke and then pretend to be asleep when the others come to bed. I am not very popular with the other Maids at the moment and think it best to keep out of the way.

I did not have long to wait to test the first of my suspects. After dinner, I accompanied the other Maids and Mrs. Champernowne to attend the Queen in her Presence Chamber. In honour of the Banoo we were to be entertained with poetry reading by Sir Edward Dyer and other members of the Court who fancy themselves poets. I hoped the Queen would read some of her own. She writes the most beautiful poems.

We were just starting up the stairs from the Great Hall when Faruk started to come down. He bowed when he saw us. This was my chance. I felt rather guilty, but as he went past me, I stuck my foot out under the cover of my skirts. The poor young man went sprawling down the last four stairs and landed in a heap at the bottom. I ran down to him, and Mrs. Champernowne puffed after me.

"Forgive me, sir," I gasped, trying to help him up.

Faruk sat up and rubbed his elbow. "My fault entirely, my lady," he groaned politely.

"That was very clumsy, Grace!" chided Mrs. Champernowne. "How it happened, I do not know. Now hurry off to the Queen while I tend to this poor young man."

So it seems Faruk is no tumbler. Surely no one would allow themselves to be hurt thus if they could help it.

The poetry reading was long, truly long, and not by the Queen at all. It was all about Phyllis the

Shepherdess treading on flowers, with a flock of gallant sheep that leap about, and having a hard heart for men but a soft spot for her pretty flock! Would Sir Edward have made such a to-do about Phyllis if she had been looking after pigs? I wondered.

When it was finally over I could not believe that the clock had only struck two. It felt as if it should have been four at the very least! Her Majesty suggested that the Banoo might like to see her sundial in the Fountain Court. The Queen is very pleased with it, for it portrays a map of the world.

Cloaks were fetched—as it was very cold and frost still lay upon the ground—and then we all made our way down my favourite avenue, where the box hedges have been cut into the shapes of animals. It is a new fashion that has just come over from Europe.

Things could not have worked out better for me, for Anoosh was there, attending Banoo Yasmine. I wanted the opportunity to test him, but was determined to do it in a different way. Stairs had turned out to be rather dangerous and I was feeling guilty about Faruk, who seemed to be making a point of keeping out of my way. Also, I wasn't sure that Mrs. Champernowne would believe a second tripping was an accident on my part!

I was beginning to think I would not have a chance to put Anoosh to the test, when I noticed how icy the ground was a little way ahead. The fountain had splashed there and the water had frozen. Sir William Paget was escorting Lady Sarah carefully along so that she didn't slip on the icy ground, while Lady Jane had to make do with Mary Shelton's support, and was looking most put out. The ice had given me an idea for testing Anoosh. As we came to the slippery patch of ground, I stuck close by Anoosh and made great pretence of losing my balance. I am sure I must have looked like Lady Jane, who is a woeful skater and hardly ever upright on the ice. I flapped my arms and shrieked a bit and managed to shove Anoosh quite hard in the back. Then I clung to a topiary chicken and watched my handiwork.

Who would have thought that one little push could cause such mayhem!

Anoosh's legs shot out from under him and he stumbled. He struggled to right himself, in a most ungainly manner, proved utterly unable to regain his balance, and ended by sliding helplessly along the icy ground on his bum. Before Faruk could move from his path, Anoosh had crashed into him. Faruk careered into Penelope and Carmina, who in turn grabbed at Lady Jane. She and Mary Shelton promptly fell over each other and collided with Lady Sarah, who, in spite of Sir William's arm, was brought to her knees! I hoped that no one would realise who had started the slipping and sliding, but I was out of luck.

The Queen, who was behind and had seen it all, shrieked with laughter. "What a wondrous display," she chortled, turning to her guest. "My Maids of Honour have many accomplishments, Banoo Yasmine. Lady Grace is particularly skilled at ninepins. See, she has knocked them all down with one ball!"

Everybody glared at me—except Lady Jane, who had been helped up by Sir William Paget and was now clinging to his arm. Anoosh kept out of my way and looked most alarmed when I went forwards to apologise, and I had to endure Lady Sarah's complaint about my ungainliness for the rest of the walk.

I think I am winning a reputation for being the clumsiest person at Court. And—worse—Faruk and Anoosh seem to have no talent at all for tumbling, which, if true, means I cannot save Ellie from her fate!

But I have one last hope. Suppose one of them is

the thief, yet is a great dissembler! He might be so cunning that he is hiding his skill. I mean to test their climbing abilities tomorrow.

But now I can hear Mary Shelton and Lady Sarah coming to bed so I shall dive beneath my covers and start snoring!

Eleven of the clock

We are in the Great Hall with Her Majesty and the Banoo and listening to the musicians up in the gallery. Well, most of us are listening. Lady Sarah and Lady Jane are squabbling with each other quietly. Today is the eve of the feast of St. Agnes and it is said that if you go to bed without supper on this night, you will dream of the man you will marry. Both Lady Sarah and Lady Jane are laying claim to Sir William Paget and denying the other permission to have him in her dreams. I will not bother with all this silliness. I could no more miss supper than dance beautifully and, knowing my luck, I would probably dream of fat old Babak!

I am enjoying the music. We have had a lucky escape: it was nearly poetry again. Sir Edward Dyer claimed yesterday that he had many more poems (probably about Phyllis) that were certain to please his fair monarch, but even Her Majesty had had enough. He would have been better served if he had written about Fair Eliza. But I must keep to the point of this entry. I may be needed to join in with a madrigal soon.

I was awake early this morning and straight away put my mind to the problem of the theft. With every day that passes, Ellie is nearer to being convicted of a crime she did not commit, and she is relying on me.

The task I had in mind to test Anoosh and Faruk's climbing skills was a very simple one. All they had to do was climb something high and difficult. The only problem was persuading them to do it. They were avoiding me as if I had the plague. I was still wondering what I could do at breakfast, when I looked across the table and saw Lady Sarah smiling at Sir William. If persuasion is needed and young men are involved there is no one better than Lady Sarah. I decided to ask for her help as soon as I could. The only trouble was, I could not explain the real reason. I would have to trick her into helping me to trick Anoosh and Faruk! I just hoped I could keep my story straight and not get found out.

Fortune was on my side, for Her Majesty had

some matters of state to deal with and did not want to see us Maids until eleven of the clock. And the Banoo was spending the morning in her own apartments. I escaped the breakfast table before Mrs. Champernowne could find me some tedious task and went in search of Masou. I found him warming his hands at a fire in the Long Gallery.

"I need you to climb that old oak tree by the chapel," I told him. "And I wish you to place my bonnet on the tallest branch."

"I have no objection to playing 'Hunt the Hat' indoors!" he laughed. "But I have no desire to go out into the cold. What strange idea is this, Grace?"

"It is a test, you dolt!" I explained. "The two pages failed the tripping test miserably. However, if they can climb, then there is still some chance that one of them is the thief. The old oak tree has branches that start a long way from the ground. It would take some skill to get footholds in the trunk."

"I will do it for Ellie," sighed Masou. "Although from what you say, neither can be the snake man that you seek." He took the hat, wrapped his cloak around him, and set off.

I made my way to the Great Hall, where Mrs. Champernowne had gathered the Maids. They were practising dancing with some of the young gentlemen of the Court. Monsieur Danton was demonstrating some new steps with Mrs. Champernowne as his partner. I slipped in and made my way quietly to Lady Sarah, who was watching intently. I saw Mrs. Champernowne's eyes follow me as the dancing master skipped nimbly around her, flicking his feet out at every turn. It was lucky for me she couldn't move.

"Pray do not interrupt me," muttered Lady Sarah. "Lady Jane will take Sir William as her partner the minute my back is turned."

"But I need your help, Lady Sarah," I whispered, "for I am going to be in terrible trouble otherwise."

"I should think you are," sniffed Lady Sarah. "Missing Monsieur Danton's instruction, again. Where have you been?"

"Out walking Her Majesty's dogs," I said quickly. "She asked me specially. But that is why I need your help."

"Not with walking those dogs, I trust?"

"No, they are safely back on their cushions," I assured her. "But while I was out a gust of wind took my hat and blew it into an old oak by the chapel. Mrs. Champernowne will skin me alive, for it is new and I lost the last one while jumping over a stream in the Park of St. James's"—that bit was true at least—"and none of Mr. Somers's troupe are available."

"So you want me to climb a tree!" squeaked Lady Sarah.

"*Silence!*" hissed Monsieur Danton, glaring at us. "*Taisez-vous!*"

"Of course I do not want you to climb a tree," I whispered to Lady Sarah. "But I have seen Anoosh and Faruk wandering around in the corridor outside with little to do. I am sure one of them could climb the tree, but I cannot ask them for they are scared of me!"

"And with good reason!" retorted Lady Sarah. It seemed she had not forgotten about yesterday.

"You are so good at getting young men to do what you want," I pleaded. "Could you not have a word with them?"

The flattery worked immediately.

"Well, I am rather," Lady Sarah said, sounding pleased with herself.

"So you'll do it, then?"

"Oh, if I must," she sighed. "I will just tell Monsieur Danton that I must rest for a few minutes and then I will step outside and send Anoosh and Faruk to retrieve your hat. I will pretend it is my hat and then they will surely oblige. But I will not accompany them, for then I will miss the dancing and Lady Jane will get her claws into Sir William."

"What are you two whispering about?" demanded

Mrs. Champernowne. She started towards us, leaving Monsieur Danton capering about on his own.

But before we could answer, the dancing master had grasped her arm. "No, no, Madame Champernowne," he chided, steering her irritably back to her place. "You stay still while I skip. You do not speak! *Mon Dieu!*"

Mrs. Champernowne went purple, but thankfully she held her tongue and did not question us further.

As Lady Sarah was making her excuses, I went back out to the old oak. Masou had done well. My hat was lodged at the very top of the tree.

"Psst!"

I saw Masou's arm waving to me from behind a bay bush. I quickly joined him and we waited there together.

It was not long before we heard voices. There seemed to be an argument going on in the language of Sharakand, and every now and then the words "Lady Sarah" were said loud and clear. I peered out to see Anoosh and Faruk both trying to get a foothold on the tree. I wondered what Lady Sarah had told them to make them so eager to win her favour. She had probably just flashed her eyes and heaved her bosom. That seemed to work with most men!

I sauntered round the bush and greeted them as if

surprised to find them there. "What's going on?" I asked innocently.

The two pages looked at me warily. I could hardly blame them so I kept my distance.

"I am instructed by the beauteous Lady Sarah to rescue her headwear," said Anoosh nervously.

"No, it is *I* who will have the honour," argued Faruk.

"But it was I she spoke to!" insisted Anoosh.

"Until she saw that I was also present," added Faruk, through clenched teeth.

At this rate I would never get to see who was the good climber—or get my hat back! "I have an idea," I said, brightly. "The two of you could take turns and I will assure Lady Sarah that you were both most anxious to please her."

"Very well," said Anoosh, nodding.

"It is agreed," said Faruk. "I will go first!" And before Anoosh could do anything about it, Faruk was hauling himself up the trunk. He made heavy weather of it, and soon found himself lying flat on his back on the ground.

"Hah! I knew it!" exclaimed Anoosh. "Now I will show you how it should be done."

At last, I thought. I have found my thief.

Anoosh ran at the tree and gave a great leap.

A few minutes later

I had to put down my daybooke for a moment, as I was called to join the madrigal. As usual it was a dreary one. I am sure I saw a tear in the Banoo's eye when we sang about "our lost home," but mayhap it was our singing that distressed her!

Anyhow, Anoosh scrabbled at the bark of the tree, trying to get a handhold. For a moment, as he clung to the trunk, I thought he was going to succeed. But he got no further and slowly slid down to the ground. It was very difficult not to laugh.

Anoosh got to his feet and brushed leaves off his tunic. "It would seem the gods have decreed that neither of us is worthy of doing the lady Sarah's bidding," he said sadly.

"She would be better asking Sharokh," muttered Faruk, "for he is good at climbing."

I did not want to ask Sharokh. I already knew that he was agile—for I had seen him catch the pitcher of wine at the ball—but since he does not occupy the crucial room above Banoo Yasmine's, there was no point in testing him. It was all very vexing!

Anoosh and Faruk went off together, heads bowed.

As soon as they were gone, Masou sprang out of

the bush, climbed the tree like a monkey, and retrieved my hat.

"So where has that test got you, Grace?" he asked as he handed the hat to me. "I tell you they are no tumblers."

"Or climbers," I sighed. "But couldn't one of them still be a snake man?"

Masou looked doubtful. "Even if that is so, how did the thief get down to the Banoo's dressing room if he cannot climb?" he asked.

"I don't know," I replied irritably. "Mayhap he could manage it with the help of a rope. I will have to set a test to see if one of them is a snake man. What else can I do? I must find a way to prove Ellie's innocence."

I looked round me for inspiration and in the distance I noticed the old fish smokehouse with its rickety door and tall, narrow chimney. I had an idea and hastened over to investigate further. Masou followed curiously.

I tried the door and it creaked open. I do not think the smokehouse has been used since the old king's time. The floor was covered in leaves, which must have drifted in through the chimney. Masou and I crunched over them. There was a grate in the centre of the room for a fire, and hooks for the fish dangling down on chains from the ceiling. I looked up at the chimney hole. I am quite thin (Lady Sarah, who is very proud of her own ample figure, calls me a beanpole) but I would not have been able to squeeze up through it.

I tugged at Masou's sleeve. "Is that chimney about the same size as the window in the tower?" I asked.

He looked at it long and hard. "Hmmm!" he said at last. "It is about the same size, in my judgement."

"Then all we need to do is lock the door and hide the key," I decided. "We can ask Faruk and Anoosh to climb in by the chimney and thus discover whether either of them is a snake man!" I was really pleased with my idea and waited to be congratulated.

But Masou just frowned. "Why would they want to do that?" he asked.

He was right. Why would they?

"Because . . . ," I said, thinking hard, ". . . there will be something very precious inside."

"Why do you not put the Heart of Kings inside!" exclaimed Masou. "And then we can all watch the sport as they attempt to steal it."

I gave him a playful shove. "Stop your jesting," I told him. "And think on this—Anoosh and Faruk were anxious to help Lady Sarah. How much more eager would they be to serve the Queen?"

"You are surely not suggesting Her Majesty should be locked inside this old smokehouse!" Masou exclaimed in horror.

"Will you try to be serious for a moment?" I scolded. "We will simply put something in here that the Queen values highly."

"And what is that, pray?" asked Masou.

"Henri," I said smugly, "her favourite dog."

Five minutes later I was coaxing Henri inside the smokehouse. Well, I didn't really have to coax him at all. He followed me—and the big bone I was waving at him—quite happily. He settled down among the leaves and gnawed happily on the bone, while I crept out and shut the door. But when I went to lock it, I realised that there was no key!

There was nothing I could do, for I could see Masou approaching, with Faruk and Anoosh, so I stood with my back to the door. It seemed our ruse had worked. Masou had offered to show them the grounds and then brought them by the old smokehouse.

When the two pages saw me, they stopped and looked about them quickly—as if searching for another route to take.

"I am so glad you are passing," I gushed, before

they could walk away, "for a terrible thing has occurred. Her Majesty's favourite dog, little Henri, has wandered inside this smokehouse, and someone has locked the door not knowing he was there. I do not know who has the key and poor Henri is getting very agitated." I hoped they could not hear the happy sounds of "poor Henri" chewing. "It will cause Her Majesty great distress unless he is freed quickly. Can you help? She will be most grateful to anyone who rescues her dog."

I wondered what Faruk and Anoosh must think of life at Placentia Palace. It would seem that there are nothing but accidents here. I hoped they were not suspicious. Thankfully, they did not appear to be, for they stepped forwards eagerly, emboldened at the thought of winning the Queen's gratitude.

"I think the only way is to go through the chimney," I explained.

Their faces fell immediately.

"Can you not try?" Faruk asked Masou. "You are a skilful tumbler."

Masou bent down and hastily rubbed his knee. "A skilful tumbler with a bad knee, I fear," he said, wincing. "Mr. Somers has forbidden me any strenuous exercise. Her Majesty depends upon *you*."

"Then the door should be forced, perhaps?" suggested Anoosh.

"We have tried," I said quickly. "But it is stuck fast, and we cannot risk hurting the dog."

The pages looked at each other doubtfully.

I led them away from the smokehouse, turned, and indicated the chimney. "In truth, that is the only way of gaining entry," I said sorrowfully.

"It appears very small," Faruk pointed out hesitantly.

"Faruk's heart seems to fail him," put in Anoosh immediately. "I will make the rescue myself."

Masou gave him a leg up onto the domed roof and he edged towards the chimney. He peered into it and then swung his legs over the edge and started to wriggle down inside.

We watched as he huffed and puffed and slowly squeezed himself further in.

After a while he stopped and waved his arms. "I am sorry to be troubling you," he called politely, "but I think I am stuck."

"What misfortune!" said Masou, looking sympathetic. "If only this ankle—" I coughed loudly. "I mean, this *knee*, were healed, I could help. But I daren't disobey my master."

Faruk clambered up onto the roof, took hold of Anoosh under the arms, and pulled hard. Anoosh popped out, in a shower of soot.

"Be reassured," he called down to me. "I spied the Queen's dog and he looks happy enough. It seems he has found something to eat!"

"But what are we to do?" I wailed, looking pleadingly up at Faruk. "Poor Henri is a brave animal. He does not show his fear, but he will pine to death if we do not free him!" It was clear that Faruk was the only one who could possibly be the thief. I was determined to get him to do the test.

At this moment Sharokh came strolling past. He stopped in astonishment when he saw his two fellow pages perched on the smokehouse roof. "Ah! I have found you at last!" he exclaimed. "But in such a strange place. The Banoo has been calling for you both to attend her. We are to listen to music in the Great Hall."

"They must rescue the Queen's dog first," I put in hurriedly. "He is locked inside this smokehouse and the only way in is through the chimney. Anoosh got stuck, so Faruk is about to try. I hope you can spare him for a few more minutes."

"It will be quicker to do it myself," declared Sharokh, jumping nimbly onto the roof.

"Please do not trouble yourself!" I called. I did not want him to stop Faruk attempting the rescue and so ruin my test. But it was too late. Sharokh already had his head inside the chimney. I could not quite see what he was doing, but he seemed to be wriggling his shoulders in a very peculiar way. Suddenly he slithered out of our view.

"I have the dog," we heard him call from inside the smokehouse. "I will pass it up. Eurgh! Desist from licking my face, hound!"

"Do not be alarmed," I called grudgingly. "He is just thanking his rescuer."

Faruk reached into the chimney and pulled a wriggling Henri out. Gingerly he handed him to Anoosh, who passed him down to Masou. As soon as Henri was set on his feet, he rushed for the door of the smokehouse and started scraping at it. I slipped over to him and tried to hold him off with my skirts, but he was determined to get back inside to his bone. I put my hands behind me and clung to the doorknob, hoping no one would notice.

I heard the hooks clanking together. Sharokh must have been swinging on them to get back out of the chimney. A moment later he stood before me, bowing proudly. I thanked him and tried to sound gracious but I was spitting inside. Sharokh had displayed the very skills that I was looking for. If only he slept in the room above the Banoo's I would have my thief.

A faint hope dawned! I decided to try and find out exactly where Sharokh's chamber was. But I needed a good reason to ask such a strange question, of course. I thought I was really quite clever about it.

"Oh, Sharokh, the Queen will be most relieved that little Henri is safe—and most pleased with your assistance. Might I know where your chamber is situated, in case Her Majesty should choose to honour you with a message of thanks?" I inquired sweetly.

Sharokh looked very pleased with himself. "Why, certainly, my chamber is on the first floor, near that of Mr. Somers. Though I share with other pages, of course."

So his chamber is nowhere near the Banoo's apartments. He may have the skills I seek in my thief, but that is of no consequence when it seems he had not the opportunity to thieve the Heart of Kings! I sighed and thanked him, and he hurried away with Anoosh and Faruk to attend the Banoo.

Hell's teeth! I am most disheartened. Though Sharokh's arrival thwarted my attempt to test Faruk's skills as a snake man, in truth I fear Masou is right—neither Anoosh nor Faruk seems skilled enough to be the thief. And I am no closer to clearing Ellie's name.

———

I have just realised that the music must have stopped a time ago, for the whole Court is on its feet and talking about it. I hope I am not expected to say anything clever, for I did not hear one note! While everybody is milling around, I am going to slip out and see Ellie. I have no good news to give her but I will take her some food. Mistress Berry is now convinced that I am having a growth spurt and will outgrow my strength if I am not fed regularly. So she has a little something for me every time I go to the Privy Kitchen.

Nearly two of the clock, at dinner

We are all sitting at dinner and I have my daybooke in my lap. I should not really have it at table. I hope no one notices that I am doing more writing than chewing. I am sure I should be ravenous by now. Dinner is very late—after a long trek through the Glass Gallery—but I am too nervous to eat!

I had hoped that we would all be dismissed after

the music so that I could make my visits to the kitchen and to Ellie. But unfortunately, the Queen caught my eye and I had no choice but to go to her and curtsy. My heart sank, for I had nothing good to tell her.

"We spoke before of someone who has tried to capture the 'Heart' of a noble lady," she said gravely. "Has he made himself known to you, Grace?"

Her Majesty was being very clever. Anyone who overheard would think we were discussing a suitor for one of the Maids. If only I had something to tell her that would help Ellie. "I fear not, Your Majesty," I admitted. "But I gain hope that I will do so with each hour that passes."

"Mayhap you mistook your man," said the Queen, "and it is time to leave it be." Her eyes were kind, for she was telling me there was no hope for my friend.

"I pray that that time is not yet come," I murmured. I dreaded that she would tell me that my investigation must end and Ellie be punished forthwith.

"Dear Grace." Her Majesty took my hand. "Then let us say that it is not yet come but will be soon upon us. You may have a few hours more but that is all."

"Thank you, Your Majesty," I said with great relief. I did not have long but it was better than nothing.

It was with a heavy heart that I set off to see Ellie. First I went to the Privy Kitchen, where Mistress Berry pressed slices of salt beef upon me, telling me they would keep my stomach from growling until the midday meal. Then I found Masou and together we went to visit Ellie.

I gave her the slices of salt beef and Ellie fell upon them. I fear the guards may have been forgetting her meals, as she seems even hungrier than usual.

Ellie had made herself a paltry sort of nest among the discarded boxes and sparkly curtains.

"You are living like a monarch here!" laughed Masou.

"Maybe so," said Ellie dully. "But I'd sooner have the starch room floor and Mrs. Fadget's acid tongue." She looked at us both. "You've said nothing of the thief. That means you know nothing, or you'd have told it straight away."

She was so downcast. I put my arm round her. "We have tried all manner of things to flush the thief out," I said. I told her how I had knocked all the Maids over on the ice and how Faruk and Anoosh were avoiding me. Then Masou tried to entertain her with the tale of the tree as if it were one of Mr. Somers's dramatic masques. But Ellie did not even raise a smile.

"All that and still there is no one who could have taken the cursed jewel!" she sighed mournfully. "I think it must have been me after all. The Bandy bewitched me and I did it in a sort of walking dream."

"Of course you didn't, Ellie," I assured her, and sighed. "In truth, we did find one perfect suspect."

"Who?" asked Ellie. "Tell me."

"The page Sharokh is a fine climber and snake man," said Masou. "But alas, he does not occupy a chamber anywhere near the Banoo's, so it cannot be him."

To our astonishment Ellie jumped to her feet, her eyes wild and bright. "But it is him!" she cried. "It must be him. And I may yet be free!" And she collapsed on the floor and burst into tears. I began to think she was wood-wild from all her time spent in her prison. I glanced at Masou. He looked as worried as I was.

He bent down to her. "Be still, Ellie," he urged. "You will only make yourself worse by weeping."

Ellie looked up. "But you don't understand," she gulped. She was about to say more when the door burst open and two guards came in. They hauled poor Ellie to her feet.

"Beg pardon, my lady," said one of them, "but we have to take the prisoner now."

"What?" I gasped. "Where are you taking her?"

"To the cell by the guardroom at the Palace Gate," he told me.

"But that is so cold!" exclaimed Masou. "There is no glass in the windows in the guardroom cell. She will surely freeze to death."

"It's too good for the nasty little thief, in my opinion," grunted the guard, giving Ellie a violent shake. Ellie began to whimper.

"But why must she go?" I demanded as they pulled her out of the door.

"We await Her Majesty's orders," replied the guard, "and soon as they come she's off to the Clink. They know how to deal with felons there."

"But she is guilty of no crime," I protested. "At least treat her like a human and not an animal!"

The guards took no notice but dragged her away, leaving Masou and me watching helplessly.

"Let me go!" shrieked Ellie, struggling fiercely. "I've got something to tell Lady Grace. It's very important."

We ran full pelt along the passageway to catch her words.

"What is it, Ellie?" called Masou. "Speak quickly!"

"It's about Sharokh!"

"Be quiet or it will be the worse for you," the guard snapped at her.

But Ellie would not be silenced. "Sharokh *did* sleep in that room with the other pages," she yelled. They had reached the door to the Conduit Court and Ellie was being hauled through. "I am sure of it," she shouted over her shoulder, "for I saw him still abed in the morning when I went in to gather the linen! Ohhhh!" One of the guards cuffed her and the door was slammed shut.

Masou and I looked at each other in excitement.

"We have heard that Sharokh is an adept climber and seen that he is a snake man besides," I began. "If he was also sleeping in Anoosh and Faruk's chamber the night the ruby was stolen . . ."

"Then he could be the thief!" Masou finished, turning a somersault in delight.

Then I had another thought. "But there is one stumbling block," I wailed. "How do we prove Sharokh's guilt to the Queen before she gives orders for Ellie to be taken to prison?"

"There is little time," Masou said gravely. "Can you not drum up another test, my Lady Pursuivant?"

"We have tested his skills," I said. "If only we could test his honesty . . ."

"Perchance it is only the Heart of Kings that he covets," said Masou, "for surely more jewellery would have gone missing if he were just a common thief."

I stared at him. "You have it, Masou," I squealed. "You are wonderful."

"I am indeed." He grinned. "Although I do not know what has caused your admiration on this occasion. Enlighten me, dear Grace."

"We will set a trap," I told him, "so that Sharokh will steal the ruby again—and this time, we will catch him in the act!"

—

Masou ran off back to the troupe and I went in search of the Queen. If I wanted to use the Heart of Kings ruby for my trap, I needed her permission. I feared she would not agree, for it would mean taking a great risk with the precious jewel. I wondered how I could persuade her that this was the only hope of catching the real villain.

But where was the Queen? I could not find her anywhere. And every minute that went by, Ellie was nearer to being dragged off to the Clink. I ran up and down the corridors looking for someone who could help me. I knew that this morning Her Majesty had told the Court what she had planned for the rest of the morning, but then my head had been too full of tumblers and tests for me to pay any heed. As I dashed round a corner towards her private chambers, I collided with one of Mr. Secretary Cecil's clerks. He was carrying a whole mountain of papers—well, he was until I bumped into him. My reputation for clumsiness will outlive me at this rate!

The papers went everywhere and we chased them down the passage while we apologised to each other, bumped heads, and apologised again. Finally we got them into some semblance of a pile, though I fear it will take him the rest of the day to sort them all out.

"I am looking for Her Majesty on most urgent business!" I told him by way of explanation. "Do you know where she might be?"

"The whole Court has gone to visit the armouries, my lady," he told me. "The Queen wished to show the Banoo the workshops King Henry, her father, had built." He seemed anxious to leave my presence. "With your permission I will withdraw. . . ."

He bowed and scuttled away. And I headed for

the armouries. I took the short cut round the orchard and in through the low door that led to the workshops.

"Greetings, Your Ladyship," came a voice. It was Jacob Halder, one of the armoury workers. I grinned. I have known him all my life. He was a very skilful man and proud of his work. I wished I had time to see what he was up to.

"Good morning, Jacob," I said. "Do you know where the Queen's party has gone? I was told they were at the armouries. I am tardy, as you see."

"Late for Her Majesty?" chuckled Jacob, wiping his brow. "That will never do! Do not distress yourself, my lady. They passed through here not five minutes since, and I heard they were on their way to the Tilting Yard, where the armour for the horses will be displayed." He sighed. "That Banoo Yasmine is a most gracious lady. She told me how she had seen armour made for olifants!"

So here was another who had fallen under the Banoo's spell!

"Thank you, Jacob," I said hurriedly, and left the workshop, picking up my skirts and running along the gravel path. I knew Mrs. Champernowne would disapprove of such unladylike behaviour but I had no time to lose. As I passed the blacksmith's forge, I heard a hubbub of voices coming from the Tilting Yard. I ran down the little alley beyond the forge and remembered, just in time, to slow down and walk sedately as I came into view of the Queen.

The Tilting Yard was full of people. And in the middle of them all stood a huge and very patient warhorse, clad in shining armour.

I pushed through the crowd until I got to Her Majesty. My lord the Earl of Leicester was showing Her Majesty and Banoo Yasmine the horse's beautifully decorated chamfron, which protected its whole head. I could see Sharokh hovering nearby. I knew I must not make him suspicious.

"Your Majesty," I said, pushing through the crowd and curtsying low in front of her, "may I beg a private word with you?"

"A private word? Here, Lady Grace?" said the Queen, raising her eyebrows and looking round at the milling courtiers. "You jest, surely!"

"Indeed not," I said earnestly. "It is a matter of the 'Heart' and therefore most serious and privy!"

"Come with me, Grace," said the Queen, catching my meaning immediately. "Let us walk the length of the Tilting Yard." She turned to the Earl. "I would ask you to entertain the Banoo a little longer, Lord

Robert," she said loudly. "I have business of suitors to deal with and must have speech alone with this silly maid!"

She took my arm and marched me away. I saw Lady Jane and Lady Sarah looking and whispering to each other and knew that I would have to invent a very rich suitor to answer the questions they were sure to ask later.

As soon as the Queen and I were out of earshot I told her what I had discovered.

"So you think Sharokh is the real felon!" exclaimed Her Majesty. "But how did Ellie come to have the Heart of Kings about her?"

"I believe that Sharokh hid the jewel in his shirt, meaning to escape with it when he could. But after his nightly exertions he overslept, and Ellie unwittingly collected it in the laundry," I explained.

"So far the villain has got away with it," the Queen remarked. "This is not to be borne! I will not have a thief lurking freely about my Court. But I and my Privy Council must have proof before Mr. Hatton's guards can arrest him. What can be done?"

"I have put my mind to nothing else," I replied, "for it is my dearest wish to see Ellie free. And I am sure that our only hope lies in Sharokh's desire to have the ruby."

"So you have a plan," said the Queen with a knowing smile. "And I can see that you are bursting to tell me of it!"

"Indeed I am, Your Majesty," I said eagerly. "With your permission, we will put it about that the jewel needs cleaning. I will make sure word reaches Sharokh that the Heart of Kings has been carelessly left in an empty chamber without a guard."

"This sounds a risky plan, Grace," said Her Majesty disapprovingly. "I cannot jeopardise the safety of the jewel a second time."

"But the ruby *will* be safe," I assured her, "for, if you will permit it, Mr. Hatton's guards will have been instructed to keep vigil close by, but out of sight. They will arrest Sharokh in the very act of stealing the Heart of Kings."

We reached the end of the Tilting Yard and the Queen stopped. "I am not convinced," she said, twisting the rings on her gloves. "If anything goes wrong, the Banoo will hardly place her trust in me again. And soon the whole of Europe will know of it!"

"Would you have them know that the just are punished and the unjust go free in this kingdom?" I asked before I could stop myself. "Forgive me, Your

Majesty," I added quickly. "I spoke in haste. But I beg you to agree to my plan. This is my only chance to save Ellie and discover the guilty party." I fell to my knees and tears came to my eyes. I could not bear to think of the fate that awaited my friend.

But the Queen simply turned and began to pace up and down, deep in thought. After what seemed a lifetime, she came back to me and held out her hand. "Arise, Grace," she said briskly. "Look, you have muddied your kirtle!"

I scrambled to my feet, though I could not have cared less about my kirtle.

"I will give this plan my blessing," the Queen said, "for I would have the real thief caught. But there are two conditions."

"Anything, Your Majesty," I managed to gasp.

"For the first, the news of the unguarded jewel must reach Sharokh's ears alone. That will protect the Court from unkind words about lax security!"

"I will make sure of it," I said, my heart singing.

"And for the second," continued the Queen, and she looked me straight in the eye, "you must promise to be well away from the chamber, Grace. Sharokh may prove violent when he discovers he is surrounded by guards, and I would not have you there.

You have been hurt serving me in the past and it is not to happen again."

I had to agree, for Ellie's sake, and I will keep my promise. But as the Queen's Lady Pursuivant, it is hard that I will not be there when the true thief is apprehended.

"I will speak to Mr. Hatton directly," said the Queen, as we walked back towards the waiting courtiers. "Now, let me think. It must not be too easy for the thief to escape, so I've a fancy to have the ruby placed in the top chamber of the west tower here." She made a small gesture towards one of the towers that King Henry had built in the Tilting Yard. "My father intended them for storming in mock combat. Let us see if your man can storm one of them single-handed! Now I shall dismiss you, Grace, so you may plant your little seed of gossip swiftly."

"I will, Your Majesty!" I promised.

As we neared the waiting Court, the Queen turned to me and her face suddenly looked thunderous. What in God's heaven had I done? I wondered fearfully, and in such a short time.

"You can forget all thoughts of marrying this clay-brained coxcomb!" she roared. "I will hear no more of the matter. Now get you gone!" I ran off with my hands over my face to disguise my huge grin! Truly Her Majesty is the best actor I have ever seen. If she were not our ruler—and if she were a man, of course—she would be the most famed player in the land.

I didn't run far. I lurked round the corner and waited, for I needed an accomplice. Soon the Queen and the Banoo and the rest of the Court passed by. I could hear Lady Jane and Lady Sarah muttering about my supposed suitor as they passed. At last Mary Shelton appeared.

"Mary!" I whispered, grabbing her sleeve and pulling her into the shadows. "I need you."

"But, Grace," protested Mary, "if it is about your admirer, I cannot help you. We all heard Her Majesty forbid you to have anything to do with him." She grinned. "Who is it, anyway?"

"Mary!" I exclaimed. "You know me better than that. My suitor is Lord Nobody, as usual! This is much more important."

Mary nodded. "So is it the secret business you have with the Queen? I wager you are still trying to clear Ellie's name!"

"That is why I need your help," I told her urgently, "for I believe I am close to doing so."

"I am glad of it," said Mary, smiling. "I never

believed poor Ellie Bunting to have any harm in her. Do you know who is the real thief?"

"I believe it to be the Banoo's page, Sharokh. And you are going to help me prove it."

"What do you want me to do?" demanded Mary eagerly.

"It is very simple," I said. "We needs must gossip!" I told Mary my plan as we walked along behind the party.

"Where is Her Majesty going now?" I asked quickly, as we joined the crowd. "I hope it is somewhere we can get near Sharokh."

"We are going to the Glass Gallery," said Mary patiently. "If you had been listening when the Queen announced her plans you'd have remembered. She has promised to show the Banoo the painting of her father meeting Emperor Maximilian. She has had it hung in the Glass Gallery, for the many windows there give good light."

—

I had never seen so many people in the Glass Gallery and began to despair. "How are we ever going to find a moment when Sharokh is alone?" I groaned.

"We may be lucky," said Mary, always the optimist.

We hung about while courtiers, who have seen the painting often before, slowly processed in front of it, pretending to view it for the first time. At last the crowd began to move off, for it was nearly one and time to dine.

But Anoosh, Faruk, and Sharokh had waited their turn to see the painting and seemed very interested in the battle scene in the background.

"'Tis a pity Sharokh's two companions are here," whispered Mary. "This would be the perfect opportunity else."

"Leave it to me," I muttered. I knew exactly how to get rid of them. "Anoosh! Faruk!" I cried, stepping towards them with a merry wave.

The two pages turned, saw who it was, and fled without a word. At last Sharokh was on his own, still engrossed in the painting.

I nudged Mary and we began to walk past. "It is scarcely to be credited," I said loudly, as if in the middle of a conversation. "The Heart of Kings left unguarded—and just for a cleaning!"

Out of the corner of my eye I thought I saw Sharokh stiffen.

"But there is no danger, Grace," answered Mary, "for surely the ruby is safe, high in the west tower by the Tilting Yard. And remember, the thief is caught and locked away."

"You are right," I said. "In any case, the jewel will not be there for long."

"And no one knows but you and I," Mary finished, "so all is well."

We hurried off before we gave ourselves away, for we were both near to giggling!

—

So now the trap is set! It is hard that I cannot go near the Tilting Yard, but I have given the Queen my word and I mean to keep it. I have had Sharokh in my sights since the Glass Gallery and all through the long meal. Every time he leans forward to take something to eat, or stands to attend the Banoo, I jump in my seat. I fear people will think I have St. Vitus' Dance or some other terrible twitching disease! Of course, I know that Sharokh cannot just leave the room—but if he is as cunning as I believe he is, he could make any manner of clever excuses to go. And yet he sits there, eating and talking as if he hasn't a care in the world.

Now I begin to doubt myself. Perhaps I am wrong and he is not the thief at all. This waiting is terrible.

It has been a most exciting day!

As soon as I could I sneaked away from the dinner table and came back to my chamber to hide my day-booke. Then I wandered about the room, waiting for news of Sharokh and the Heart of Kings. I tried filling the time with some embroidery—poor Robin Redbreast has been much neglected—but I could not concentrate. Then Lady Sarah and Lady Jane came in, united in their nosiness.

"You are a dark horse, Lady Grace Cavendish," chirped Lady Sarah. "Who is this young man that the Queen so disapproves of?"

"I am not telling you!" I said. I wished they would go away.

"I warrant it is young Toby Pikelet," sniggered Lady Jane. "He would like a better position at Court, but has no patron."

"And no chin, either!" put in Lady Sarah.

"I will tell you my secret," I said sweetly. "It is Sir William Paget. I am thinking of missing supper tonight so that I can dream of him in honour of St. Agnes's Eve."

Both my fine ladies stopped their tittering at that. Lady Sarah gasped, while Lady Jane cast me a look that held many a dagger. Then, without another word, they both swept out of the chamber. I was left in peace.

Except I could find no peace. I walked up and down. Then I gazed out of the window to see if there was any river traffic. Then I counted the crests on my bedcover. I got to two hundred and fifty-six and gave up. This was hopeless. I decided I would go for a walk around the grounds. So long as I stayed away from the tower by the Tilting Yard, I would not be breaking my promise to the Queen. I put on my warmest cloak and gloves.

As I walked down the corridor I suddenly had a thought. I could pay an innocent visit to the Banoo's apartments. That way I could at least find out if Sharokh was there.

—

My knock on the door was answered by Esther, who ushered me in. The Banoo was most gracious about my visit.

"I am pleased to see you, Grace," she said, with a huge smile. "You are always welcome here. Come, sit with me. Esther will bring us some ale."

Esther bowed and withdrew.

As we spoke I cast a furtive look round the long chamber. I could see Anoosh and Faruk at the far end. They were engrossed in a game of chess and had not noticed me. Many of the Banoo's other servants were also there—but not Sharokh. He was nowhere to be seen! I felt my heart race and tried to concentrate on telling the Banoo all about skating and how I had only just learnt the skill. She was fascinated and wanted to know more, but all the time I was thinking about Sharokh. What was he up to at that moment?

There was a scratching at the door that led to Rajah's chamber. In my nervous state I had forgotten about the panther.

"Rajah is awake," said the Banoo with a smile. "I expect you would like to see him, would you not, Grace?" She motioned to Anoosh, who jumped up and went to fetch Rajah.

"Come, my prince," called Banoo Yasmine, holding out a hand to the panther. He trotted over and laid his huge head on her palm, looking up at her with devotion. Then he came over to me and rubbed against me like a cat wanting milk. He nearly pushed me off my cushion!

"What a life he leads," laughed Esther, returning with the ale. "He has eaten well and slept for several hours. Now all he requires is to stretch his legs."

"May I take him outside, Banoo Yasmine?" I

gasped. After all, I had thought of walking in the grounds, and Rajah's company would certainly help take my mind off Sharokh and the Heart of Kings.

"That is an excellent notion," said the Banoo. "I can tell that Rajah likes you and will do your bidding. Won't you, my darling?" She kneaded the fur between his ears, which he obviously liked, for he closed his eyes and made a deep purring sound.

I got the most curious looks as I led Rajah through the passageways of the palace on our way to the gardens. He padded nobly along, with his head held high. Most of the courtiers had never been this near to the panther, and some of them did not look as if they liked it much, either! But after a while I realised I could have recommended walking Rajah to Lady Jane and Lady Sarah. Many of the young men who saw us couldn't wait to show how bold they were and I got more attention than I had ever had from them before. Actually it was the panther they made a fuss of, which suited me very well, but doubtless those two fine ladies would have turned it to their advantage. Perhaps I will suggest it to them and see what they say!

A river mist had come up since this morning and the air felt very cold and damp as we went out into the knot garden. Rajah pulled on his leash as soon as he scented the outdoor smells. He went round every bush, sniffing keenly. I think he had picked up the scent left by something small and tasty-smelling—which probably meant one of the Queen's dogs! And I doubt he had ever seen or smelt fog before.

I wondered what was happening at the Tilting Yard. Surely by now Sharokh must have made his attempt. With any luck, Mr. Hatton had him in chains and the ruby was locked safely away again.

I was itching to make for the Tilting Yard and find out, but I knew I mustn't, so I took Rajah in the opposite direction through the palace gardens. We came to the door in the wall that led to the kitchen garden of the old friary. I knew that Rajah and I would be able to run round the garden if there was no one else there, and the guard at the door was very quick to let me through when he saw my companion.

There were pockets of mist hanging in the air and I could only just see the opposite wall of the overgrown kitchen garden, and the spire of St. Alfege's church in the village beyond. I was glad to have Rajah's company, for the garden felt eerie in the fog.

We were just picking our way over some fallen fruit canes when Rajah stopped and lifted his head.

His keen ears had heard something I had not. I wondered if there was someone in the garden that I could not see. Or perhaps it was just a bird. Then I heard it, too—the sound of running feet. It seemed to be coming from somewhere in the palace gardens.

To my surprise, Rajah began to pull me along the wall towards the far end of the garden. He must have keen sight, for he had definitely spied something. He began to give little eager chirrups of pleasure.

Suddenly the mist cleared in front of me, and now I could see what Rajah had spotted. A figure had appeared on top of the high wall near the end of the garden. He ran nimbly along the narrow bricks with no thought that he was at least fifteen feet from the ground. I recognised who it was and my heart began to pound. It was Sharokh! He must have escaped from the guards.

"Down, Rajah!" I whispered, laying my hand on his head and praying he would obey. He seemed most eager to run and greet Sharokh, but I wanted to stay hidden. I remembered how keen Rajah had been to play with Sharokh in the Banoo's chambers—and how terrified of the panther Sharokh had been at the time. Thankfully, Rajah lay down at my bidding and I crouched beside him. I hoped we were hidden by the mist and the tangle of forgotten black-berry bushes.

Now I could hear the sounds of pursuit.

"Someone get up there after him!" came the voice of Mr. Hatton from the other side of the wall.

"The men have tried, sir," somebody answered. "It is too high!"

"Then shoot him down!" ordered Mr. Hatton.

Sharokh immediately leaped off the wall into the kitchen garden and landed with a swift forward roll, not far from where I was hiding!

I heard Mr. Hatton give an oath. "Quickly!" he called. "You two stay here in case he comes back this side. The rest—follow me to the door."

I heard running footsteps as the guards rushed towards the door where I had entered. But it would take them a few moments, and Sharokh was now back on his feet and heading for the opposite wall. That way led to Greenwich Village and the river, with its many escape routes. Mr. Hatton and his men would never arrive in time to cut Sharokh off. The plan had gone horribly wrong! Sharokh was going to make off with the Heart of Kings!

Rajah stood up and pulled forwards with a whine. And suddenly I knew what to do. It was so simple. I let go of the leash!

With a happy roar, Rajah bounded joyfully towards Sharokh. Sharokh turned and screamed in terror. I imagine all he could see was the huge black shape of the Banoo's panther flying towards him out of the mist. Rajah knocked him to the ground, stood on his chest, and began to lick his face.

After a few moments, Mr. Hatton and his men came panting up. They slid to a halt at the sight of the felon, felled by a Maid of Honour and a panther! One of them nearly dropped the torch he was carrying.

"Well, my lady," said Mr. Hatton, wiping his brow. "You seem to have caught the miscreant with the help of that . . . creature. We had him cornered in the tower, with the jewel in his hand. But somehow he slipped from our grasp."

"Witchcraft!" muttered one of the guards. A look from Mr. Hatton silenced him.

"We have now but to put him in chains and recover the ruby," Mr. Hatton finished.

Rajah was nuzzling Sharokh's hair and purring loudly. "Help me!" whimpered the page. "Get this devil cat off me, I beseech you."

The Gentlemen of the Guard looked at each other. None seemed keen to do as Sharokh asked.

Mr. Hatton cleared his throat. "I wonder, Lady

Grace," he said, sounding rather ill at ease. "If you have any power over the beast, perhaps you could use it now, so that we can make our arrest."

I found it difficult to keep my face straight. There stood a lot of grown men in breastplates and not one would go near the panther. They must have thought Rajah had attacked his victim.

I stood over Sharokh and looked down on him. "I will call the panther off," I told him, "when you have given me the Heart of Kings."

Sharokh's eyes were wide with fright. Slowly he inched a hand down towards his belt and pulled off a leather purse. Without a word, he nudged it across the ground towards me. I picked it up and opened it. There inside was a ruby. But I wanted to be sure it was the Banoo's gem. I held it up to the light of the guards' flaming torches and saw the twelve-pointed Star of Karim deep within. This was indeed the Heart of Kings! I bent down and took Rajah's leash. "If you make any move to escape," I told Sharokh, "then I will release the panther again. And we have proved that he can run faster than you!"

Ten minutes later I stood in the Presence Chamber. The Queen sat with the Banoo next to her. On the Banoo's lap was the casket containing the precious ruby. Sharokh knelt in front of them, his head bowed. He was flanked by Banoo Yasmine's two guards. They looked as if they wanted to kill him there and then. Mr. Hatton's guards were at the door, but they needn't have been there at all. Sharokh was not going anywhere, for I was holding the panther's leash!

The Queen fixed Sharokh with a furious glare. "Explain yourself, you miserable wretch!" she demanded.

Sharokh raised his head. "I humbly beg forgiveness," he bleated. "It wasn't me. It was Ashraf, the new king. He forced me!"

"Threatening you with great wealth, I imagine!" said the Banoo scornfully.

"No indeed, my lady!" whimpered Sharokh. He began to speak rapidly in his own language.

"Enough!" ordered the Banoo. "You will speak in English. Your actions have been insult enough to her Gracious Majesty."

"Do not make things worse for yourself, man!" snapped the Queen.

"I meant no disrespect, Your Esteemed Majesty," said Sharokh. "The truth is this. Ashraf sent a messenger to me before we fled. He told me that he must have the jewel, or the people would not accept him as king. The messenger said I was to get it for him or I would be killed. I refused. I asked, Why me? Ashraf's followers are many—they could seize the jewel at any time. But the messenger, he said Banoo Yasmine is a clever woman. If she received knowledge of any plot to take the Heart of Kings she would destroy it."

I heard Esther gasp in horror.

"That I would never do," murmured the Banoo gravely. She took the precious jewel from its casket and held it up so it flashed in the candlelight. "This ruby is the most powerful symbol of our monarchy. If I believed Ashraf to be the rightful king and not the murdering usurper that he is, I would have given him the jewel gladly. But see, it is still here, Sharokh. It has shown its power and protected itself from theft. The Heart of Kings chose its protectors wisely." She looked at Rajah and me and smiled.

I felt very proud and I am sure Rajah did, too—although he hid it well by having a good scratch.

"Merciful Banoo," wailed Sharokh. "Have pity on your loyal servant. I have profited nothing from this and put my life in great danger."

"It is not for me to judge," Banoo Yasmine told him coldly. "We are in England and under the rule of its noble monarch."

I began to feel sorry for poor Sharokh. It sounded as if he had had no choice. He had been threatened by Ashraf. I hoped Her Majesty would be lenient with him.

But then the doors at the end of the chamber were flung open. The guards moved aside as Babak entered. He had a cloth bag in his hand and he looked very flustered. He bowed low before the Queen.

"What is the matter, sir?" asked Her Majesty. "For your face seems to hold news that your mouth would speak of without delay."

"Great Majesty!" panted Babak. "Forgive the intrusion, Wise Ruler, but I found this among Sharokh's possessions."

Sharokh turned white. "That is not mine," he shouted. "I have never seen it before!"

"And yet it does hold a vast sum of Sharakand gold . . . ," said Babak.

"I do not have any gold," broke in Sharokh. "It must belong to another."

". . . and a small key curiously similar to that which opens the casket for the Heart of Kings," Babak continued.

"I . . . ah . . . I . . . ," Sharokh stammered, at a loss for words.

I saw Esther's eyes widen in amazement and relief.

Clearly, Sharokh had had his own copy of the casket key. Esther had not left the casket unlocked, after all.

But Babak hadn't finished. "And, lastly," he said, "this document giving you, Sharokh, safe passage back to our homeland. It is signed by"—Babak turned and spat on the floor in disgust—"Ashraf, so-called King of Sharakand, may he rot in hell."

Sharokh was silent.

The Queen stood up. She was very calm but her eyes flashed with fury. "Take this worm from our sight," she commanded. "He will enjoy our hospitality at the Tower—but not as one of our treasures!"

Members of the Gentlemen of the Guard stepped forwards and dragged Sharokh away.

"Mr. Hatton," said the Queen. "Send a man directly to release the laundrymaid. Have her present herself at the Privy Kitchen for a good meal, and have Mrs. Fadget informed that Ellie Bunting is innocent, but will not be able to return to her duties until she has recovered from this ordeal."

It was as much as I could do not to drop Rajah's leash and go with the guard. I had almost made up my mind to ask permission to withdraw, when the Banoo stood up and turned to the Queen.

"I am saddened that I have brought this disgrace

to your Court, Gracious Majesty," she said. She held out the casket. "I do hope you will again receive the Heart of Kings as surety. I know it will be safe, locked in your Tower of London."

"The whole sorry matter is behind us, Banoo Yasmine," said the Queen, smiling. She handed the casket to Mr. Hatton and then put her arm through the Banoo's. "Come, my dear, we will arrange the ruby's journey to its vault. Then much preparation must be made, for I have a mind to feast well tonight. And perhaps we will have you dancing the volta!" Then she turned to the panther. "And I believe that you, Master Rajah, shall have a special supper tonight of finest venison, in recognition of your loyalty to us."

As soon as I could I made straight for the Privy Kitchen. There was no sign of Ellie, but Mistress Berry threw her arms in the air.

"Lord bless us, Lady Grace!" she declared. "Have you an identical twin? For if not, you eat a prodigious amount of food!"

"I am not here to eat," I assured her. "But I have good tidings. Ellie Bunting has been released, for the real thief is captured! Ellie is to be brought here for a meal, and she will be mightily hungry."

I wondered what Mistress Berry would do, for she had had some hard words to say when she thought Ellie a felon. But it seemed her memory was short.

"Oh, I'm that glad!" She beamed. "She's a good girl, that Ellie Bunting, and I won't have a word said against her. Tabitha! Fetch some broth."

With Mistress Berry on her side, Ellie's reputation will soon be restored, and I know Masou will also spread the news of her innocence. Of course, Mrs. Fadget may still be unkind, but then Mrs. Fadget always is!

At that moment, Ellie was ushered in. She looked ready to faint and I ran to her and helped her to a bench. Mistress Berry flapped around, bringing her broth and bread and cheese and apples, and a little mead to drink.

"For you are too thin by half," she told Ellie. "Now, eat up before you faint from hunger. You've been given a great honour—allowed in the Queen's own kitchen!"

At last she bustled away and we could speak freely.

"Ellie!" I gasped. "I am so pleased to see you."

"I thought I'd never set eyes on you again, Grace," said Ellie weakly, in between spoonfuls of broth. "I believed it was the end for me when they

169

took me to that horrible guardhouse. I warrant I'll be having nightmares." She looked happily at the food in front of her. "Though it feels like I've come from hell to heaven!"

"I'm so glad it is all over," I said, wishing there was no one in the kitchen so that I could give her a hug.

"And it's all thanks to you," Ellie said with a smile. "Mr. Twyer, the guard, told me all about how you and the panther caught that Sharokh." She gulped some mead and wiped her mouth. "It proves one thing," she told me. "That ruby is cursed, like I told you."

"What do you mean?" I asked.

"Well, Sharokh meant it ill and he got his punishment!"

"I'm not so sure," I said. "He would have escaped if he had not minded being licked by a friendly panther. I think his fate was in his own hands."

"No, it was the ruby," Ellie insisted, nodding. "Else why would he be on his way to the Tower?"

I could not answer that one. Perhaps Ellie was right.

"Ellie, my favourite little laundrymaid!" It was Masou. He turned cartwheels around the table, much to Mistress Berry's horror and Ellie's delight.

"I'm so glad my efforts were not in vain and you are now free!"

I looked at him.

"I had a little help from Grace, of course!" he added cheekily.

"And don't forget Rajah!" I reminded him.

"Yes, the two of you did well," he said seriously. "I don't know what I would have done if anything had befallen my friend Ellie." He made as if to take her hand but instead pinched some pieces of bread from her trencher and began to juggle them.

"You give them back," Ellie said in mock indignation. "That's my dinner you're playing with."

And it was probably one of the best dinners Ellie had ever had. What a shame that she had to be nearly taken off to the Clink in order to deserve it!

"Grace," came a voice from the door. Mary Shelton stood there. "The Queen wants you, now! She's in her Privy Chamber. You'd better not delay."

I gave Ellie's hand a quick squeeze and followed Mary to the Queen.

As soon as Her Majesty saw me at the door of the Privy Chamber, she ushered everybody out in an impatient manner. Several courtiers gave me sympathetic glances. When Her Majesty clears a room, it usually means a tirade is about to follow. And this suited the Queen's purpose well—no one would have guessed she wanted a quiet word with her Lady Pursuivant.

"So you have thwarted another villain, Grace," she said with a smile, as I curtsied in front of her, "and proved the innocence of our little laundrymaid. Your loyalty to the great and the humble does you much credit. 'Tis a pity that in matters of state, the humble are sometimes but ants trodden upon unnoticed."

I knew that this was the nearest Ellie would get to an apology for her false imprisonment.

"I am deeply thankful that Ellie wasn't trodden on in the end!" I declared.

"And I am thankful that you were not harmed in any way," said the Queen. "It seems I may make any rule I wish to keep you safe, and yet trouble seeks you out!"

"I swear I followed your orders, Your Majesty!" I assured her.

"I know it," said the Queen. "I should have ordered Sharokh to stay away from *you*." She offered me a sugared fruit from a bowl by her side. Then she looked at me and her eyes sparkled. "A happy ending, my dear. And now you may go. We are heartily glad that there are no more thieves abroad in the palace, thanks to your efforts. At least we can be sure that if we turn our back, no little thing will be taken— such as, perchance, these sugared fruits, which are so popular with a certain laundrymaid. . . ." And she turned her back on me and the sugared fruits.

I took the hint, sneaked up to the bowl, filled my hands with sweet delicacies for Ellie, and made silently for the door.

As I left, I heard the Queen roaring with laughter.

Almain—a stately sixteenth-century dance

bodice—the top part of a woman's dress

bum—bottom

bumroll—a sausage-shaped piece of padding worn round the hips to make them look bigger

casement—a window

casket—a small decorative box

chamfron—a piece of armour for a horse's head

chemise—a loose shirtlike undergarment

the Clink—a prison in Southwark, especially famous in Tudor times, and one of the earliest prisons in England

clothes press—a large storage cupboard

comfit—a sugar-coated sweet containing a nut or seed

damask—a beautiful, self-patterned silk cloth woven in Flanders. It originally came from Damascus— hence the name.

daybooke—a book in which you would record your sins each day so that you could pray about them. The idea of keeping a diary or journal grew out of this. Grace is using her daybooke as a journal.

doublet—a close-fitting padded jacket worn by men

dulcimer—a stringed instrument

false front—a pretty piece of material sewn to the front of a plain petticoat so it could be shown under the kirtle

farthingale—a bell- or barrel-shaped petticoat held out with hoops of whalebone

gossamer—a fine, filmy cobweb

harbinger—somebody who went ahead to announce the monarch

hose—tight-fitting cloth trousers worn by men

jerkin—a close-fitting, hip-length, usually sleeveless jacket

kirtle—the skirt section of an Elizabethan dress

kohl—black eye makeup

Lady-in-Waiting—one of the ladies who helped to look after the Queen and who kept her company

lead—lead carbonate, used for makeup

madrigals—beautiful part-songs, which were very fashionable

Maid of Honour—a younger girl who helped to look after the Queen like a Lady-in-Waiting

manchet bread—white bread

marchpane—marzipan

Margaret of Angoulême—queen consort of Henry II of Navarre and sister of King Francis I of France, Margaret was a very influential woman and famous for her writings and her interest in religion.

Mary Shelton—one of Queen Elizabeth's Maids of Honour (a Maid of Honour of this name really did exist). Most Maids of Honour were not officially "ladies" (like Lady Grace), but they had to be born of gentry.

masque—a masquerade, a masked ball

olifant—an elephant

palliasse—a thin mattress

partlet—a very fine embroidered false top, which covered just the shoulders and the upper chest

pavane—a slow and stately dance

penner—a small leather case that would be attached to a belt. It was used for holding quills, ink, knife, and any other equipment needed for writing.

plague—a virulent disease that killed thousands

posset—a hot drink made from sweetened and spiced milk curdled with ale or wine

Presence Chamber—the room where Queen Elizabeth would receive people

pursuivant—one who pursues someone else

Queen's Guard—more commonly known as the

Gentlemen Pensioners, young noblemen who protected the Queen from physical attacks

retinue—the group of aides and retainers attending an
important person

scullion boy—a servant employed to do rough kitchen
work

Secretary Cecil—William Cecil, an administrator for
the Queen (later made Lord Burghley)

Shaitan—the Islamic word for Satan, though it means
a trickster and a liar rather than the ultimate evil

stays—the boned laced bodice worn around the body
under the clothes. Victorians called it a corset.

stomacher—a heavily embroidered or jeweled piece
for the center front of a bodice

St. Vitus' Dance—a nervous disorder, associated with
rheumatic fever, which caused fast, jerky, uncon-
trollable body movements

usurper—someone who seizes something without
authority

Tilting Yard—an area where knights in armor would
joust or "tilt" (i.e., ride at each other on horseback
with lances)

tiring woman—a woman who helped a lady to dress

trencher—a wooden platter

tumbler—an acrobat

vellum—fine parchment made from animal skin

volta—a sixteenth-century dance very popular with Queen Elizabeth I

White Tower—the oldest part of the Tower of London

Withdrawing Chamber—the Queen's private room

wood-wild—crazy, mad

A NOTE ABOUT JEWELS

During Elizabethan times, jewels were just as prized as they are today. In fact, sometimes a nobleperson would use jewels instead of money to purchase very expensive items or to cover a debt.

If you look at any portrait of Queen Elizabeth I, you will see that she was painted wearing many beautiful jewels. Such extravagant jewelry indicated to anybody viewing the portrait that she was a rich and powerful ruler. Rumor had it that as the Queen grew older, she liked to be painted with more and more impressive and elaborate jewelry. Apparently, she thought the splendid gems would attract people's attention and keep them from noticing how her face was aging!

But jewels weren't just impressive decorations. They had symbolic meanings, too. In several state portraits, the Queen is shown wearing a jeweled pelican. This symbolized the Queen's selfless love for her people, because the pelican was known to pierce its own breast with its beak in order to draw blood with which to feed its babies.

Often the Queen wore pearls—these symbolized her virginity and purity and were extremely fashionable at the time. She famously bought a string of pearls that had belonged to her cousin, Mary Queen of Scots, for what was said to be a bargain price of £3000. In Elizabeth's time, £3000 was more like several million dollars today—some bargain! However, pearls were the Queen's favorite jewels, so perhaps she felt they were worth it.

In the "Armada portrait," created to celebrate the famous English victory over the Spanish Armada in 1588, you can see a beautiful pearl necklace around the Queen's neck. This was reportedly the last gift that Robert Dudley, Earl of Leicester, the Queen's favorite courtier (see *Conspiracy*), gave to Queen Elizabeth I before his death later that same year.

Who knows whether something as extraordinary and magical as the Heart of Kings ever existed? But jewels remain an important symbol of the monarchy today. The Crown Jewels, kept in the Tower of London, include several gems as fabled as the Heart of Kings. For example, legend has it that the Koh-i-noor diamond ("Koh-i-noor" means "mountain of light")—now part of the Queen Mother's Crown—will bring its male owners nothing but misfortune, while a woman who wears it will rule the world. No doubt Queen Elizabeth I would have liked to own that!

In 1485, Queen Elizabeth I's grandfather, Henry Tudor, won the battle of Bosworth Field against Richard III and took the throne of England. He was known as Henry VII. He had two sons, Arthur and Henry. Arthur died while still a boy, so when Henry VII died in 1509, Elizabeth's father came to the throne and England got an eighth king called Henry—the notorious one who had six wives.

Wife number one—Catherine of Aragon—gave Henry one daughter called Mary (who was brought up as a Catholic) but no living sons. To Henry VIII this was a disaster, because nobody believed a queen could ever govern England. He needed a male heir.

Henry wanted to divorce Catherine so he could marry his pregnant mistress, Anne Boleyn. The Pope, the head of the Catholic Church, wouldn't allow him to annul his marriage, so Henry broke with the Catholic Church and set up the Protestant

Church of England—or the Episcopal Church, as it's known in the United States.

Wife number two—Anne Boleyn—gave Henry another daughter, Elizabeth (who was brought up as a Protestant). When Anne then miscarried a baby boy, Henry decided he'd better get somebody new, so he accused Anne of infidelity and had her executed.

Wife number three—Jane Seymour—gave Henry a son called Edward and died of childbed fever a couple of weeks later.

Wife number four—Anne of Cleves—had no children. It was a diplomatic marriage and Henry didn't fancy her, so she agreed to a divorce (wouldn't you?).

Wife number five—Catherine Howard—had no children, either. Like Anne Boleyn, she was accused of infidelity and executed.

Wife number six—Catherine Parr—also had no children. She did manage to outlive Henry, though, but only by the skin of her teeth. Nice guy, eh?

Henry VIII died in 1547, and in accordance with the rules of primogeniture (whereby the firstborn son inherits from his father), the person who succeeded him was the boy Edward. He became Edward

VI. He was strongly Protestant but died young, in 1553.

Next came Catherine of Aragon's daughter, Mary, who became Mary I, known as Bloody Mary. She was strongly Catholic, married Philip II of Spain in a diplomatic match, but died childless five years later. She also burned a lot of Protestants for the good of their souls.

Finally, in 1558, Elizabeth came to the throne. She reigned until her death in 1603. She played the marriage game—that is, she kept a lot of important and influential men hanging on in hopes of marrying her—for a long time. At one time it looked as if she would marry her favorite, Robert Dudley, Earl of Leicester. She didn't, though, and I think she probably never intended to get married—would you, if you'd had a dad like hers? So she never had any children.

She was an extraordinary and brilliant woman, and during her reign, England first started to become important as a world power. Sir Francis Drake sailed round the world—raiding the Spanish colonies of South America for loot as he went. And one of Elizabeth's favorite courtiers, Sir Walter Raleigh, tried to plant the first English colony in North

America—at the site of Roanoke in 1585. It failed, but the idea stuck.

The Spanish King Philip II tried to conquer England in 1588. He sent a huge fleet of 150 ships, known as the Invincible Armada, to do it. It failed miserably—defeated by Drake at the head of the English fleet—and most of the ships were wrecked trying to sail home. There were many other great Elizabethans, too—including William Shakespeare and Christopher Marlowe.

After her death, Elizabeth was succeeded by James VI of Scotland, who became James I of England and Scotland. He was almost the last eligible person available! He was the son of Mary, Queen of Scots, who was Elizabeth's cousin, via Henry VIII's sister.

James's son was Charles I—the king who was beheaded after losing the English Civil War.

This story about Lady Grace Cavendish is set in the year 1570, when Elizabeth was not yet thirty-seven and still playing the marriage game for all she was worth. The Ladies-in-Waiting and Maids of Honor at her Court weren't servants—they were companions and friends, supplied from upper-class families. Not all of them were officially "Ladies"—

only those with titled husbands or fathers; in fact, many of them were unmarried younger daughters sent to Court to find themselves a nice rich lord to marry.

All the Lady Grace Mysteries are invented, but some of the characters in the stories are real people—Queen Elizabeth herself, of course, and Mrs. Champernowne and Mary Shelton as well. There never was a Lady Grace Cavendish (as far as we know!)—but there were plenty of girls like her at Elizabeth's Court. The real Mary Shelton foolishly made fun of the Queen herself on one occasion—and got slapped in the face by Elizabeth for her trouble! But most of the time, the Queen seems to have been protective of and kind to her Maids of Honor. She was very strict about boyfriends, though. There was one simple rule for boyfriends in those days: you couldn't have one. No boyfriends at all. You would get married to a person your parents chose for you and that was that. Of course, the girls often had other ideas!

Later on in her reign, the Queen had a full-scale secret service run by her great spymaster, Sir Francis Walsingham. His men, who hunted down priests and assassins, were called Pursuivants. There are also tantalizing hints that Elizabeth may have had her own personal sources of information—she certainly was very well informed, even when her counselors tried to keep her in the dark. And who knows whom she might have recruited to find things out for her? There may even have been a Lady Grace Cavendish, after all!

Be on the lookout

for the next

Lady Grace Mystery,

FEUD

on sale
October 2006.
Turn the page for a special preview.

Feud

I think that was a wonderful morning, no matter what Lady Sarah might think. Mrs. Champernowne left as soon as Sarah was ready in the Queen's robes, which are most magnificent in black and white velvet and brocade, and heavy with pearls and jewels of all kinds.

The five painter-stainers were preparing their palettes with odd-smelling pigments. They all wore brown smudged smocks to protect their clothes. Three were quite old—at least forty!—Another was very old and grey, and the last was Nick Hilliard, who is tall and slim but has the remains of a black eye.

I happen to know he got it in a tavern brawl ten days ago because Ellie told me all about it. She heard of it from one of the other laundrymaids who knows a lad who works in the stable, who has a friend in the smithy whose brother was in the tavern when Nick got the black eye. She said that Nick was boasting of all the money he would make—because he has next to none at present—when he got himself a patron with his latest great Classical painting. One of the other card-players said he couldn't wait that long for his money, and Nick said he didn't pay cheats! So the other man hit him and there was a big brawl, which broke up the game. And that was just as well, Ellie said, because the cards were marked and Nick was too drunk to know it. "An' it served him right to get his eye blacked," she added darkly, "for not knowing what a terrible coney-catcher that man is and 'ow you shouldn't play him at anything—'specially not cards and dice."

I glanced cautiously at Nick, who looked well-enough for a drinking man.

He caught me looking at him and smiled ruefully, touching his cheekbone. "Do you like my battle scar, my lady?" he asked.

"I heard you got it in a fight over a card game," I said. "Is that true?"

"In a way," he admitted. "Lord knows, some men get very impatient for their money. Do you like to play?"

"I play a little Primero with the Queen some-times," I told him. "But she generally gives me the money to play in the first place."

He smiled again, and shook his head. "But where's the excitement in that," he asked, "if you can afford to lose?"

I didn't know what to say to that.

Lady Sarah, who was perched on a stool on the lit-tle dais, sighed, and I remembered I was supposed to be reading to her. I had a new book about brave war-riors and magical lands and a quest for a magic sword.

Mrs. Teerlinc went to her desk in the corner and began to cast up her accounts with an abacus and a long list of bills. I tried to watch her as I read aloud, attempting to learn how she could write accounts with pen and ink and not get ink on her at all.

Mrs. Teerlinc is the Head Limner at Court and has a pension from the Queen, so all the other limners are jealous of her, especially as she is a woman. Because of her position she has little time for actual painting, so she mainly creates beautiful, tiny portraits and pictures on vellum stuck to playing cards.

It's the latest thing to have a miniature portrait of your love to carry with you. Daft gentlemen are always saying they want to carry Lady Sarah's beauteous visage next their devoted hearts. Ha!

I tried to concentrate on reading. The book is translated from the French and has some very long words in it. I quite like romances, if only they could get to the fighting sooner and leave out some of the description of the beauteous lady's golden locks, wondrous samite gowns, and tiny feet clad in Cordova leather and so on. Of course, Lady Sarah loves those parts.

I read and read, but I also kept looking up to see Nick Hilliard painting. It is interesting, for he is intent, like a cat watching a bird before pouncing, and his hand moves so fast with the brush, it is as if he can't paint fast enough to catch the colours in front of him.

Lady Sarah was scowling at me, her cheeks pink from wearing the Queen's heavy robes, and I realised that watching Nick Hilliard had stopped me from reading. So I started again hastily.

"You've read that bit," she snapped crossly. "Twice!"

I coughed, skipped a paragraph, and read on. One of the stainers tutted because Sarah started fanning herself with the Queen's ostrich fan instead of staying still.

Mrs. Teerlinc had finished her accounts and now had her hand on the shoulder of the stainer who was painting nearest to me. He was an old man with a tangled grey beard and eyebrows like birds' nests. He squinted at Sarah and then squinted up close to the panel he was painting, as if he could hardly see what he was doing. I thought the pupils of his eyes looked odd, as if there was milk in them.

"I think you should rest your eyes now, Ned," said Mrs. Teerlinc. "You go for your pipe and a bit to eat."

"Ay, well," he said. "My eyes are tired. Maybe the morning mist will have cleared when I come back." He cleaned his fingers on a rag, tucked the brushes into the easel so they wouldn't touch anything else, and went out of the Workroom.

Mrs. Teerlinc looked at his painting and sighed. "Nick, my dear," she said sadly, examining some mistakes in Ned's painting, "would you mind?"

Nick came over from his own easel, bringing his palette and brushes. He scowled at Ned's painting. Then he grabbed a brush and painted like lightning, right over Ned's mistakes—which you can do with paints that are mixed with oil, for they don't run at all.

And the result was so much better. As Nick used his colours and lit the sheen of the pearls with silver in resin, the jewels seemed to grow there on the panel, hanging on the bodice like the real jewels!

"Oh, really, Grace," snapped Sarah, "Please will you stop *stopping*?"

Guiltily, I returned to reading some elaborate speeches about lady-loves while occasionally sneaking glances at Nick Hilliard's work.

I read about the terrible dragon and the beauteous lady in its clutches, and I tried to concentrate, but every so often I'd forget to read as I watched jewels and brocade spring up from Nick's brushes as if burning through the wood panel.

By the time Ned came back, smelling of that

horrible hensbane of Peru that some people smoke to cure their phlegm, Nick had finished reworking all that the old man had done that morning and was back at his own easel, looking as if butter wouldn't melt in his mouth.

I remembered Mary Shelton's embroidery pattern and forgot all about reading again. "May I have some heavy paper for pouncing an embroidery pattern for Mary Shelton?" I asked.

"Of course," said Mrs. Teerlinc, and she beckoned one of the two apprentices to bring some scrap paper to me. "You Maids certainly do a great deal of embroidery work," she added.

"Well, it is the only way we can make pictures with colours," I explained, a little sadly, for I would love to do some painting myself. "I wish I could learn to paint with the beautiful, bright colours you use."

Mrs. Teerlinc smiled and shook her head. "Ah, no," she said. "I'm afraid they are too valuable. The blue for the sky is made of ground lapis lazuli. Besides, it takes years to learn how to use all the colours. And at least embroidery silks will not stain your kirtle."

"No, thank the Lord, or I would never have a clean one!" I declared ruefully. "I have trouble enough with pen and ink."

"Grace," moaned Sarah. "What happens next? Stop chatting about drawing and painting and read to me."

But Mrs. Teerlinc was patting my arm. "Perhaps I can help," she said. "Here is a graphite pen—see, it makes only a grey dust if you brush it. You can write with it and never need to dip your pen in an ink bottle."

"How wonderful!" I exclaimed. "It would be marvellous not having to use ink." Of course I tried it—and that is what I am writing with now! No ink at all!

"You can draw with it, too," Mrs. Teerlinc added with a smile, and gave me two more graphite pens from her little table, which I put straight in my penner. "Now, be careful with them, for they are quite easy to break and *very* expensive, so I will not be able to give you more."

"*Gra-a-ace!*" moaned Sarah once more. "What happens with the dragon?"

So I sat there for another hour, burbling speeches from the beauteous damsel, and even more speeches from the brave knight who rescued her.

At last the Queen's kirtle was done and we could leave. I helped Sarah change her clothes again—it's lucky she doesn't mind doing that, at least. It is terribly fiddly: lifting off the heavy gown and putting it on its stand, unlacing the sleeves and drawing them off, unhooking the bodice down the side, and then unhooking the back of the kirtle and drawing that off. Finally, I untied the Queen's stay laces so Sarah could stand in her shift and bumroll and farthingale and sigh and breathe again. And then, of course, I had to do her up again in her own stays and bodice and kirtle. It's agonisingly boring, wearing fine clothes, really it is. I wish I were like Ellie and could put one thing on in the morning and wear it all day. In fact, I don't think she even puts it on in the morning. I think she just wears it day and night until it falls apart or she grows out of it and has to find a new kirtle.

I went back to the parlour for a bite of dinner with Lady Sarah. Olwen was waiting for us, and Sarah decided I hadn't been very good as a tiring woman, so after we ate, she had Olwen dress her all over again. But the good thing was that I managed to sneak a little time in my chamber to try out my new graphite pen. And so here I am, and this pen is a wonder of the world, for it never blots nor runs at all!

Mary Shelton has just come in from visiting Carmina, who has a terrible megrim, poor soul, and was not with us for dinner. "Penelope says there is to be a play tonight in honour of the Scottish Ambassadors!" Mary has just said excitedly. "And Her Majesty desires you to walk the dogs, Lady Grace."

So, off I go.